The Village Girl

Emily Khalayi Wekulo

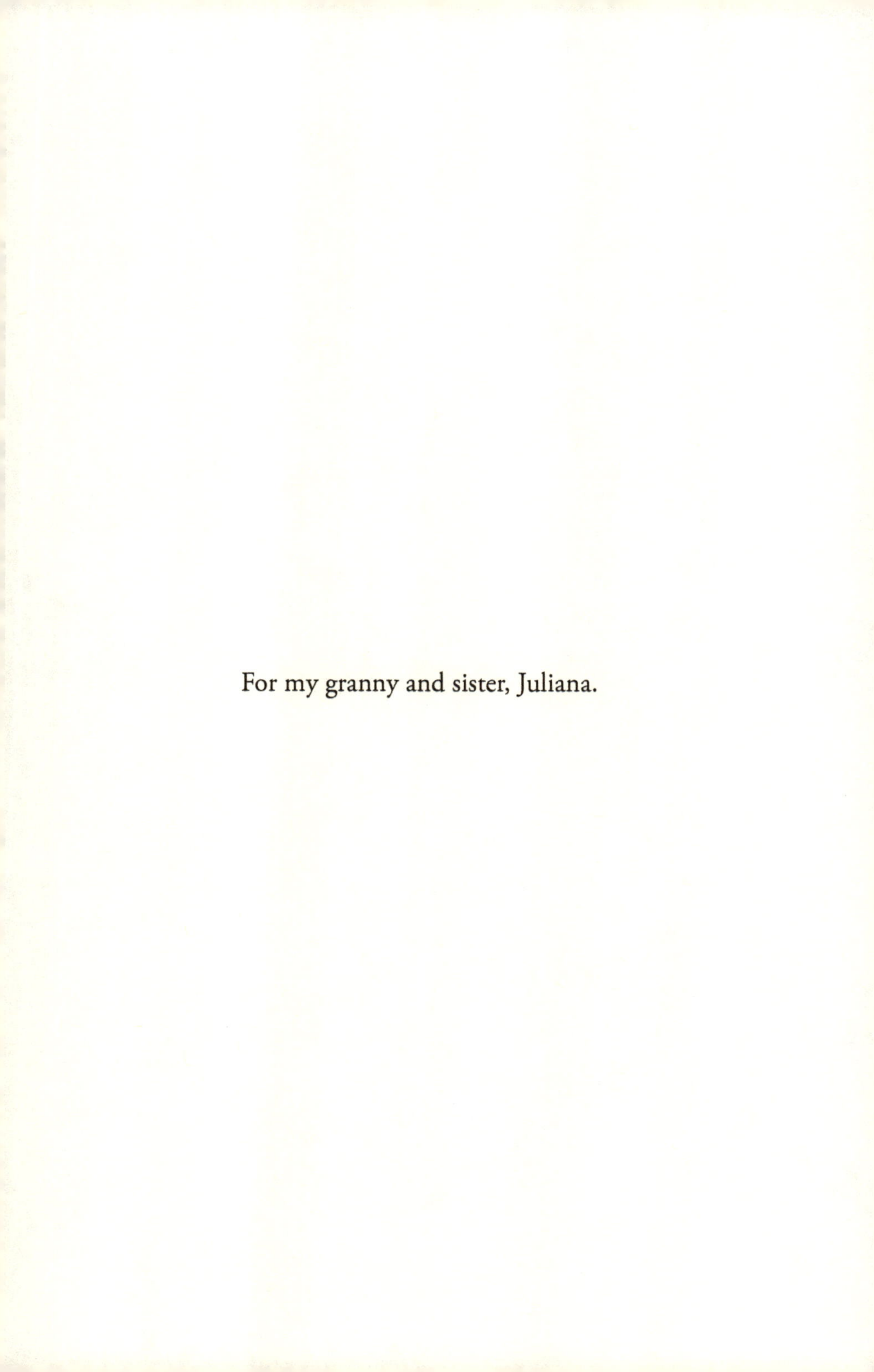

For my granny and sister, Juliana.

CHAPTER ONE

It Takes a Whole Village to Raise a Child.

Smoke rose through grass-thatched roofs of huts that littered the village, lazily towards the sky like monstrous snakes. The crackling sound of the morning fires that greedily licked the blackened soot filled many huts. The aromas of tea and porridge - breakfast for school going children and working husbands- rented the air. Women fed the fire with more wood as children scrubbed their cracked heels on stones. The children winced at painful bites of frozen water on their goose-pimply skins. The sun struggled behind thick greyish clouds, forcing its rays past tall planted and short indigenous trees that sprayed deep green colors all over the village, competing for attention with vast sugarcane plantations and the evergreen grass. Dust settled on the main road and small split paths that penetrated into homesteads. Viewed from atop a tree like many small boys do, the village looked like a giant palm of a hand with many fingers.

This was an ordinary morning for Nakhumicha. She had woken up and warmed her belly with the sugarless porridge that she made herself. Then, she smoothed her heels on a rock that sat at the center of her grandmother's compound. Afterwards, she smeared her feet, hands, and face with milking jelly- Arimis, and waded through the dewy grass with the rest of the children, headed to school.

Nakhumicha was happy with herself. She had already split the firewood for granny and fetched a few liters of water from the river for the cows and granny's bath later in the day. She had even cleaned her sleeping patch after letting the chicken out. Nakhumicha knew that granny would be happy when she woke up. Nakhumicha had no parents she knew of. However, it didn't bother her. She had her grandmother, and the old woman meant the world to her.

The old woman turned every stone around in her house to ensure that Nakhumicha was raised well and provided for. With the help of the Catholic Church and the rest of the village women folk, the old woman had witnessed her grandchild transform from a toddler to a playful girl, and now Nakhumicha was speeding towards teenhood.

Rumor had it that Masafu, the bang vendor was the young girl's father, and some women amid their fits of laughter and loud talk, dropped hints every time they saw Nakhumicha at the river. She ignored them and convinced herself that Masafu could not be her father. She made up a story about her father dying in the city where her mother was and told it to all the young girls in her school several times until she believed it herself. Only her best friend, Timina, knew the truth.

Like many other small girls in the village, Nakhumicha and Timina stayed away from Masafu. After all, it was said that in his big, bloodshot eyes there was a trap that drew small and older girls into his half-mudded hut or sugarcane plantations where he devoured them. He would then threaten to kill them and the rest of their families if they dared tell anyone what he did to them. Most of his victims remained silent, walked with a limp along the far end of the road with their eyes fixed on the ground, and, even worse, attempted suicide. For older girls, their mothers took them to the village doctor, Takitare Wasilwa, later locking themselves in the house for a week and emerging looking thinner and pale, with an escort of whispers behind their backs. Such girls would disappear from the village to go to their relatives' places in other villages or in the city and only come back when there was a new unfortunate girl to talk about.

Everyone was afraid of Masafu. The police could not arrest him. It was rumored that he had a stepbrother in the city, who was a senior government official. The hushed whispers said Masafu sent his stepbrother many kilos of bang to sell in the city and therefore was protected from the top. Masafu walked around the village, swaggering in arrogance and pride, his huge chest popping out of the tight cheap football club jerseys he donned over baggy, jeans trousers with very large pockets.

As Nakhumicha briskly walked to school, routinely, in front of her walked the children of businessmen, nurses, teachers, and secretaries in the village paper mill. All the children in front of her ran to the gated Catholic school. Behind her stayed the children of peasants, farmers, orphans, out-growers, stepchildren, and drunkards. Like an unruly swarm of flies, they buzzed towards the gateless Catholic public school. Nakhumicha ran faster to ensure that they stayed behind her, ignoring the prick and pressure of the stones on her bare feet and the dust that was making its way inside her patched green, pink-sleeved school tunic. By her side was her hope of seeing her mother one day, owning a bed in a room with no smelly chicken and having shoes. The other children tried catching up, so she ran faster and only slowed down when she sensed Timina behind her.

The sun had succeeded in going past the clouds, pouring forth its warmth onto the shivering children. This reduced the clatter of teeth and heightened the fear of arriving to school late. After all, this would mean a visit with Mr. Mangicholi, the fierce deputy headteacher who split their small backsides with cypress canes. The children dreaded him not because he caned them but because all of the parents asked him to do it. They told him not to spare any child who misbehaved, and when he started whacking them, he enjoyed every whack and smack that he brought down on the culprit. The victims squirmed and screamed while the others huddled in a corner, trembling with fear and swearing that they would never do anything wrong in school.

Nakhumicha had never been a victim of Mr. Mangicholi's lashes since she started school. She ensured that she was among the first to cross the stones that acted as the school's gate, and that she stayed above average in mathematics- Mr. Mangicholi's subject. Nakhumicha was always quiet in class, afraid of ending up on the list of noisemakers. Timina, on the other hand, was good at doing exactly what Nakhumicha did, including re-writing her answers during exams. Timina often copied everything, including Nakhumicha's name. She only got lucky when Nakhumicha spotted her name in Timina's answers and elbowed her hard so that she could realize her mistake and correct it.

As the two girls settled on the wooden desk and took out their half-cut exercise books simultaneously. Nakhumicha felt the warm roast sweet potato in her sling bag. It would serve as her break-time snack. Her stomach rumbled like a distant thunder roll in response, causing Timina to give her a familiar look that said, 'I am hungry too.'

Similar days went by, with the two girls loving each other, sharing roast maize and sweet potatoes, loving science and religious studies, struggling in Kiswahili and Mathematics, bewildered in English, and feeling nothing at all in Social studies. Their similarities of being fatherless, both staying with their grandmothers and loving similar subjects glued them together. The trips to the river, to the forest for firewood, to school and church made the duo inseparable.

CHAPTER TWO

Danger and Delight Grow on the Same Stalk.

Nakhumicha's heart thumped softly inside the bony cage that rested beneath her chocolaty skin that afternoon. She stared into the horizon; her eyes glued on a feathery cloud. Above her, a yellow and grey robin nested on the tree that she loved sitting under. It was a huge Meru oak that defied age and weather- always leafy and very green. The trunk was a mutilated whitish grey thick stalk that curved like a sculpture. Its branches shot too soon from the fat stalk, making the tree short and thick, with a shadow that covered three-quarters of her grandmother's compound. The grass beneath Nakhumicha was soft and pillow-like, kind on her bottom.

On such afternoons, Nakhumicha often sang her favorite "Mama Maria" song, wondering how Mary got pregnant by the power of the Holy Spirit. She would stare at the horizon and speculate: *Is the Holy Spirit human? What did the priest mean by saying the angel of God came over Mary? Did the same angel come over my mother before she was born? How come Masafu is my father? How did Masafu become my Father? I envy Jesus for being the Child of the Holy Spirit and Joseph. He has two fathers, yet I have none!*

Today, Nakhumicha was not thinking about Mary with her two baby daddies. Instead, she was thinking about herself. Her chest had started sticking out, forming two tiny domes beneath the silky blouse she was wearing. Every time she tried pushing it back, the soft mounds stayed vigilant on her chest, like two soldiers on watch. She felt bad about them. She did not like the soreness and the fact that no other girl in her class had domes on their chests. The bigger girls in senior classes had them, and every time they ran, the domes bounced up and down on their chests like tennis balls. Nakhumicha had never made fun of the older girls like the other small girls did. *Why is my chest growing bigger? What had I done to deserve this punishment from God?* Nakhumicha tried going through her mind to see if there were traces of her making fun of an older girl or any other crime, but she found none.

The small hills on her chest had come with a new attitude in Granny. She recently began telling her, "Nakhumicha, you've become a woman. But if you let boys play with you, you will get pregnant."

The small girls in her school never went near boys. Only the bigger girls giggled on the road when boys walked behind them. The thought of the proverbial ogres that turned into handsome boys and men- only to trap girls and devour them later, as told by her Granny, chilled her. Behind every handsome face, she saw a three-eyed ogre, breathing fire and swallowing girls whole.

Nakhumicha had never dreamt of playing with boys, but Granny kept pointing out that she should be careful. So, under the leafy tree, she decided that she would never take off her sweater. Nakhumicha also settled on the fact that the small hills on her chest would be a source of trouble for the rest of her life. Nakhumicha decided to keep them to herself and stay away from boys forever. She hated what she had become: the girl with a growing chest who should never go near boys.

As days went by, her woes with her growing breasts multiplied. Wambulwa, the village bushy-eyed-beast, had made a face at her one morning when she was coming from the river. Wambulwa was like the ogre in her grandmother's tales. Both men and women were afraid of him. He was the tallest creature Nakhumicha had ever seen. When she met him that morning, he was heading towards the water dam, *'Mwitisi'* and Nakhumicha was coming from there. Instinctively she moved towards the hedge to let the giant pass. Luckily, there was an elderly woman behind her, so her fear was halved.

The road was lined with bushes, melting into sugarcane forests, which cast shadows across the road, making it eerie every time even Nakhumicha walked there, even if the sun was high. Wambulwa had walked towards her, making her squeeze herself against the bushes. His eyes were fixed on Nakhumicha's chest. As he walked closer, like a gigantic spider trying to catch a fly, slowly, Nakhumicha's heart raced. The water was splashing on her from above, making her blouse wet and sticky.

"*Wambulwa, olaminilanga omwana mumusiru sina mala engila yabalaile busa?*" The voice said behind her startled them both.

(Wambulwa, why are you squeezing that child into the bushes, yet the road is wide enough for you to pass?)

Wambulwa moved away from Nakhumicha, after he had winked at her. The events of that morning chilled her. Nakhumicha hated her chest and wanted to rub herself on the rough bark of the tree, to try and make her breasts disappear. She knew they were the same reason Wambulwa had tried to come towards her.

Meanwhile, Nakhumicha's best friend Timina was lucky. Her chest remained flat. She did not have to worry about anything. She could pass near a boy without being afraid. Nakhumicha started to notice that boys struggled to pass near her, and they would intentionally try to touch her breasts. Her anxiety grew every day, with the growth of her two bad-luck mounds on her chest. Granny pumped the 'being a woman' talk in her head every day, warning her against being like her mother.

"If you let boys play with you, you will end up like your mother!" Granny would remark harshly.

Nakhumicha felt embarrassed. She did not want to breathe the same air as boys, sit in the same class as boys or stand near a boy in the assembly. She wore a T-shirt under her uniform and a sweater on top every day, every time. She hated her new life and wanted to go back to being a little girl. She wanted to be young; someone who could run without objects bouncing on her chest. She hated being a big girl, and the fact that Timina remained a small girl made her sadder.

Nakhumicha stood up to drag herself to the kitchen, to cook the vegetables Granny had instructed her to cook before she left for her Saturday Legion of Mary meeting at church. Nakhumicha wondered what she would wear to church the following day. Her Sunday best dress was growing tight around the chest. She wished she could just get sick to avoid going to church. As she blew in the fire, sending sparks all over the tiny kitchen, Wambulwa's face floated in front of her. She stepped back, staggered to a corner and rubbed her eyes with the back of her hand. More faces floated in front of her. They were faces of boys in her class, and they were winking at her. Each face mutated into a huge hand, and they were trying to touch her breasts. A small cry escaped her mouth, and she sunk on her knees, allowing tears to flow.

Chinyenyi Chayile?" (Are the vegetables ready?) Her grandmother's voice brought her back from her trance.

Nakhumicha had not even mounted the pot on the dying fire. Smelling trouble, she remained silent and rushed to put the pot on the fire.

CHAPTER THREE

If You Don't Know Where You Are Going, Any Road Will Take You There...

Sundays were always beautiful. Nakhumicha's grandmother woke up very early, prepared tea, and would add a few granules of sugar. Sunday was the only day Nakhumicha drunk milk tea with sugar. This particular Sunday, Granny had boiled some sweet potatoes to accompany the sweet tea. Nakhumicha was happy with breakfast but sad with herself. Her head had a distant throb, and none of her Sunday clothes hid the mounds on her chest. Granny had frowned at the blouse she was wearing and told her, "Wear something that fits you well." Nakhumicha had no idea what that would be, since everything seemed smaller, and there were no new handouts from the convent for needy children.

"We are getting late!" Granny shouted on her way out. Nakhumicha forced herself into the white T-shirt that felt tight around the chest, a black pleated skirt that swallowed the whole lower part of her body and rushed barefooted after her grandmother. She breathed in a heavy sigh when she finally found a spot to sit in the church. It always overflowed with congregants.

The village Catholic church was a mixture of pink, blue and golden yellow. The huge table that was fitted across the altar imprisoned the priest and the altar boys. The altar was covered in draping white with drops of green, purple or red, depending on time of the year. This was the purple time of Lent, when Christ was about to be crucified. On the wall right behind the huge table, was a golden chest with an ever-burning light. It was believed that as long the light stayed lit, the body of Christ was present.

Nakhumicha sat there, listening to Father Ekisa read through the Gospel according to John. Nakhumicha asked herself, *Why does Father Ekisa use the same flat and low voice from the beginning of the mass to the end? He talks like he has many sacraments stuck in his throat.* Father Ekisa was the only Priest serving the two masses. He also managed the Catholic Schools with the help of the nuns who always looked sad and shook people's hands like their fingers would break. They also talked softly and walked with a rosary everywhere.

One day, Granny told Nakhumicha to work hard in school so that she could become a nun like those ones. Nakhumicha had been horrified. She did not want to be a nun. She wanted to be a lawyer. She did not want to wear the baggy, dull-colored habits with a veil on her head for the rest of her life. Granny told her to be a nun with a smile of admiration on her face. But Nakhumicha had smiled in disgust and rebellion in return. Granny did not see that, because she was busy staring at the nun who was softly talking to an elderly woman who belonged to the Legion of Mary.

"Twaeni mule nyote, huu ni mwili wangu utakao tolewa kwa ajili yenu na kwa ajili ya wote..." Father Ekisa's nasal

voice read the invitation to the table of Christ. This made Nakhumicha snap into attention.

The distant throb she had in her head that morning was getting louder. She felt like her breaths were getting stuck in her nose. Nakhumicha shook the feeling away and stood up to join the queue to get her share of the body of Christ. Nakhumicha wanted to avoid going, but the thought spending the rest of the evening receiving a lecture on sin and how Christ died to save the sinners was not what she wanted that Sunday. In a stoop, she walked to the altar where Father Ekisa, stood in purple robes and a white skirt. He looked like a big purple bird preparing to fly.

"*Mwili wa Kristo?*" Father Ekisa asked through the nose.

Nakhumicha whispered, "*Amina,*" and stuck her tongue out at the sacrament like a chameleon catching a fly. When Father Ekisa placed the body of Christ on her tongue, it made her so queasy. She was not sure if it was the finger that brushed her lip or her throbbing head. She even made the sign of the cross with her left hand. Her stomach was turning and churning, making her feel the bits of tea mixed in with sweet potatoes hit the walls of her tummy. Nakhumicha felt the contents rise in her throat, making tears of panic roll down her face. She bumped into Rosalia, the hefty woman who always sung loudly with an open mouth. Rosalia had no molars or premolars. An awful smell hit Nakhumicha's face, making her convulse, struggling to keep the contents in her throat lower.

The women who were shrilling in crescendos of Eucharist songs started whispering and pointing at her. Their whispers floated in the thick warm air that was suffocating her and got stuck inside her ears.

"*Huyu mtoto ako na kitu…*" One whispered loudly.

Nakhumicha did not turn to see who it was. Instead, her mind was focused on getting away from the church, to the fences where she could spill out the bitter liquid in her throat. The hot yellow liquid shot out of her mouth with the sacrament, sending her into convulsions as she struggled to push out coagulated tea and sweet potatoes. The children playing outside the church swarmed towards her. Her head was spinning. Nakhumicha tried walking away from them, but the tiny faces floated in front of her like little demons, mocking her. Nakhumicha's head felt heavier on her shoulders. She just needed someone to help her carry it or just lay it down. Her tears defied her efforts of making them stop so she gave up and allowed a flood of mucus and tears wash down her face.

As Nakhumicha walked on, the mid-morning sun glared at her, frying her brown skin and making it sticky. She was frantically looking for a place to lie down. She forced herself into a bush and laid down on her stomach, letting her heavy throbbing head rest on her folded arms.

CHAPTER FOUR

A Burnt Child Dreads the Fire...

Her nostrils stung, forcing a sneeze that sent her head into a new wild blaze. She sat up, looked around her, straightened her skirt, and tried to stand up. Her vision was blurry. She rubbed the back of her hand across her swollen eyes, making them clear. The sun was setting, and darkness struggled to overpower the little light that was left by the sinking azure ball. She was scared.

Nakhumicha had laid in the bushes for almost five hours. Her breath was hot, and her body sticky. Her limbs were weak. The fear of being far from home in the dark gave her the strength to push herself all the way to her grandmother's house. She was worried about her grandmother. *Who had cooked lunch for her? Had the calf been watered? Was there firewood?* She knew that Granny must be worried about her, so she hurried home, ignoring the throb in her head.

Nakhumicha did not know what was wrong with her. She just felt very sick. She went through the opening that acted as a gate on her grandmother's compound and walked straight to the kitchen. There was a fire and a pot bubbling on it. Granny was not in the kitchen.

"You are still too young, your chest is barely bumpy, yet you are already misbehaving?" Granny screamed at her back.

Nakhumicha was startled. She turned around, awakening the stinging bees in her head. She shut her eyes, letting tears flow.

"Why are you crying? You little ungrateful invalid! After all the trouble I have gone through for you, this is how you repay me? You are worse than your mother!" Granny went on.

Nakhumicha could not understand what Granny was talking about. She had not walked anywhere except school, the river, church, and to the forest to look for fire. She was not like her mother. She tried convincing herself amid the rants and the abuses of Granny. Nakhumicha closed her eyes tight and stood still waiting for her to stop, so that she can could beg for Panadol.

"Who is the father?" Granny barked at her.

Nakhumicha's eyes opened with her mouth simultaneously. *Which father is Granny talking about?* She wanted to ask but her throat was dry. She tried to swallow saliva, but she had none in her mouth. It felt like a dry wind had blown into her mouth. She just stared at the semi-toothless small, almost wizened woman vibrating in anger. Granny grabbed her. She started raining blows on her, beating every part that was accessible on her body. Granny picked a large piece of wood from the bunch of split firewood that lay on the ground and started working on her legs, hands, head, and back. Nakhumicha tried running, but her feet could not let her. She thought that she would die. She screamed, begged, and convinced her Granny, but the old woman refused to hear her.

Granny was shouting, reminding her, "I took care of you! Your mother left. You have embarrassed me." Nakhumicha did not know what she had done. *Was it because I vomited in church?* Nakhumicha was one of the girls who volunteered to clean every Sunday, and she had not remained to do it. *Is that why Granny is angry?* Nakhumicha stopped screaming and struggling. She lay prostrated on the ground and waited for the blows to come down. She felt herself breathe out hotly. Then, the beating was less painful. The darkness hung deep inside her head. Nakhumicha started feeling like she was falling into an endless pit. The pain was going through her ears, making her gasp for breath. The fire in the kitchen disappeared into the darkness. Granny's voice came as whispers until finally it stopped. Nakhumicha could not feel anything anymore.

"Young girl… Young girl… Can you hear me?" A voice came to her after what felt like an eternity.

Is it God? Am I dead? Has Granny killed me? Nakhumicha tried opening her eyes. There was a strong smell of soap and detergent around her. It made her nose sting.

"Am I in hell?" Nakhumicha asked herself. *Heaven cannot smell like this. Does the devil wear spectacles?* The image of the man leaning close to her was getting clearer, and her head was now splitting again.

"My head hurts." She whispered. Nakhumicha waited to be told that she was in hell. Nakhumicha waited to be told that her sins of offending Granny would warrant her eternal burning.

"Can you sit up?" the voice asked. It was now clear. It was the doctor - Takitare Wasilwa. She was in his clinic. Nakhumicha tried sitting down, but every part of her body ached. The events of that evening came back to her. She was suddenly scared. *Where is granny?* She looked around. Her heart was racing again.

"Do you want me to call her?" the doctor asked, reading her mind. "She is sitting out there, waiting for you to get better. I am going to ask you a few questions."

Nakhumicha shook her head at Granny being called and nodded to the questions. The doctor wanted to know, "Have you started your menses?"

"No," Nakhumicha said.

"Have you been close to a boy?" asked the doctor.

Nakhumicha said, "I only see boys in school and we don't sit together."

"Are you sure?" the doctor asked, looking pointedly at her.

Nakhumicha sighed and nodded. Tears welled up in her eyes. "Granny hates me because I have these things growing on my chest," she said, sadly pointing at her chest, "Please give me medicine to take them away."

Her voice was so sad; it moved the doctor. He looked at her for a second, pitying her innocence and hating the old woman for a moment, for being so cruel.

"You don't need medicine to make them disappear. They will make you a beautiful woman in future," he said, smiling reassuringly.

The room was a splash of cream and distant green. The smell was concentrated, and it made her nose itch. The detergent welled up in her throat instead of oxygen. The wall in front of her was full of pictures of people dropping pills into wide-open mouths, coughing, children screaming at injections, and pregnant women listening to nurses. One of the diagrams fascinated her. It was a picture of a father, a very pregnant mother, and a daughter in a mosquito net. The young girl was delighted, smiling with her perfectly white teeth sparkling. The girl's hair was split at the center and tied up into two ponytails. The girl's father was tall with a clean haircut. His hand rested on the belly of the mother. The mother rested her head on the father's shoulder. They were covered in a blue mosquito net. Nakhumicha felt sadness grip her. She longed for such a family. She wished she was born somewhere else. Maybe she would not be scared of her breasts if her mother raised her.

The doctor walked away and called in her grandmother. Nakhumicha coiled farther on the small bed that she was sitting on. Her eyes were wide with fear. One look at her grandmother was enough to tell her that she was better off dead than alive. Granny's grey eyes were dark, and the veins on her forehead were pulsing. Granny shot an angry look at her and threw herself into the chair the doctor showed her.

"Mama, nimepima msichana, ako na malaria." The doctor explained to Granny. Granny's eyes narrowed then widened. Nakhumicha's eyes stayed on her folded hands. Her heart attacked her gut furiously. *I'm not sure if having malaria is a good or bad thing. Will Granny beat me up again?* Nakhumicha's eyes went back to the picture on the wall, and she wondered if the girl in the picture ever got malaria. Nakhumicha wondered if that other girl got beaten when she fell sick. Nakhumicha wished that she could ask her, but she was just a picture, and not real.

"Papa, hii pana mararia. Hii mimba papa. Angalia fisuri…" Granny said, pleading.

"Mama, mimi ndio daktari hapa. Huyu mtoto ni mdogo sana. Hajui hata mimba ni nini. Mpeleke nyumbani, na umpee hii dawa." Doctor Wasilwa said with finality, handing her three packets of drugs.

Doctor Wasilwa gave some to Nakhumicha and asked her, "Swallow." Nakhumicha did so. "Okay, Granny," the doctor said, turning over to the elderly woman. "Bring Nakhumicha something to eat. Then, take her home."

Nakhumicha was very relieved. Her throbbing head was calming down, and she could feel her swollen body slowly soothing up, with the pain leaving little by little. Her lips were cracked, and one of her eyes was bloody blue. The doctor wiped the blood from her cracked lip and covered the bruise on her cheek in a bandage. Nakhumicha wondered, *How will I go to school tomorrow? Has my best friend Timina heard anything about my ordeal?*

Granny came back with a huge bottle of Fanta. Nakhumicha's heart almost stopped when she saw bread. Soda and bread were only seen on special days like Christmas. Granny had bought her *"matiaba"*- the huge bottle. A whole bottle. Nakhumicha swallowed the mixture of orange and white greedily and chewed hard on the bread until her head started hurting again. Granny also found a motorbike to take them home.

That night, Granny let her sleep in her bed. It was small, and they squeezed in together. But it was much better than sleeping on the floor next to chicken.

The next morning, Granny did not wake her up to go to the river. Granny served her tea in bed, like a child.

Nakhumicha felt weak but Granny said, "If you eat well, you can go to school tomorrow."

Nakhumicha's wounds were covered in dark hard skin and were slowly disappearing. As she ate the sweet potato and washed it down with tea, she promised herself, *Never embarrass Granny again. I promise… I will never be anything like my mother.*

CHAPTER FIVE

Every Family Has a Skeleton in the Cupboard…

The two traumatic days were now behind Nakhumicha. She was torn between happiness and worry. She was happy because Granny had been good to her since she returned from the hospital. However Nakhumicha was worried about how she would be treated at school.

The next day, Timina was the first to receive her with a barrage of questions. Nakhumicha knew that her best friend was itching to know what the doctor had done to her. Even so, there was distress in her deep brown eyes. Timina was scared of being seen with her.

Nakhumicha looked up. The rest of their classmates were watching them. Timina noticed, gulped, retreated and moved away from her. Nakhumicha felt a pain inside her heart. She wanted to scream and say, "I don't have anything contagious!" She wanted to tell everyone, "It is Malaria!"

But there was no point. They all believed what they wanted to.

So, Nakhumicha walked away and sat on her desk, taking out a science textbook, and staring at the diagram of the digestive system. The day went by with no one talking to her. Nakhumicha ate the banana she carried with her that day alone. Nakhumicha closed her eyes to the teachers who looked at her suspiciously and shut her ears to those who talked behind her back in whispers. When the day finally came to an end, Nakhumicha ran all the way home without stopping.

Wednesday was better. Timina came to her, smiling, and extended her hand to her. They walked to school hand-in-hand.

"My grandmother said you had Malaria." Timina said, looking at Nakhumicha with blank eyes. The fear was gone—just excitement and curiosity.

"The doctor said a mosquito bit me," Nakhumicha answered with a shrug. "But now I cover my head when I sleep."

She deliberately left out the part where she slept with Granny. It would have been embarrassing that she had no bed of her own at her age.

"I have something to tell you, Micha," Timina said, using the play name she always called her. The dance in her eyes told Nakhumicha it was something big.

Unlike Nakhumicha, Timina lived with her mother and grandmother. Timina's mother worked in her salon on the market, plaiting women and girls' hair. Some paid in cash, but others paid with baskets of beans, maize, and millet. This enabled her to put Timina through school and dress her like a Chief's daughter. Timina, in return, was a good obedient daughter who never asked about her father, who ran to the river, fetched firewood, watered the calf and the chicken, and swept the floor. Timina, her mother and grandmother were a closely-knit family of three women. Timina's grandmother was very religious. She was the Mama for the Assembly of the Quakers Church. She always donned white from head to toe. She walked carefully like one afraid of hurting ants. All her talks were accompanied by, *"afume yesu"*, meaning *praise Jesus.*

Nakhumicha thought that Timina was lucky. She had her mother to take care of her. She cuddled with her mother at night. They had no enemies stalking them, and no one was courageous enough to start a bad rumor about Timina's father. Everyone knew that he had died in war, and her mother had chosen to stay with the old woman, her mother-in-law. Timina had everything that Nakhumicha dreamt of. Even so, not even once did Nakhumicha envy her friend. On the contrary, Nakhumicha was happy for her friend. She was grateful for Timina's happiness.

"What did you want to tell me?" Nakhumicha asked, dragging her friend towards the end of the field. "You know that your secret is safe with me." Nakhumicha looked at Timina with anticipation. "Yesterday, my grandmother came home with something in her bag." Timina started, "She did not want me to see it."

The dew on the grass they sat on was drying. The brittle grass beneath them was softened by the warmth of their behinds. It was sunny and warm as the two girls enjoyed their solitude, torn away from the rest of the school. Nakhumicha reached inside her blue sling bag and pulled out some roast maize, enthusiastically urging her friend to go on.

"I followed her because I thought it was bread. I suspected she did not want Mummy and I to share, like she always does." Timina obeyed Nakhumicha's eyes.

While talking, Timina also reached inside her green similar sling bag and fished our two pieces of peeled sweet potatoes. She gave one to Nakhumicha, who took it and handed Timina a piece of roast maize. Timina, at once, abandoned her piece of potato. Instead, she focused on breaking maize from the cob and throwing the grains in her mouth. Nakhumicha's eyes were stuck on the dark black-tea face of her friend with anticipation.

Timina kept going, explaining in-between chewing. "Anyways, my grandmother opened the bag and pulled out something that looked like a big belt. I thought it was a belt for her Sunday dress, but it was black. My granny never wears black."

"Was it a belt?" Nakhumicha asked impatiently. She was baffled.

"No!" cried Timina. "I tried to see it but she threw it under the bed."

Nakhumicha wanted to ask what happened next. But instead, she just let her lips quiver in anxiety and waited for her friend to go on.

"But then, the belt came crawling from under the bed." Timina said, observing as Nakhumicha raised her hands on her head and dropped her jaw.

"What kind of belt crawls? Why was your granny hiding from you?" Nakhumicha had very many questions.

Meanwhile, the field was full of children's laughter and play songs. The boys around them were howling in semi-broken voices, calling on each other to pass the ball. They did not mind the girls. The two little girls at the far end of the field were absorbed in the tale of a crawling belt. As they looked at each other, the noises made by the rest of the school came to them as whispers.

Nakhumicha was so shocked that every time she tried to open her mouth to ask a question, her mouth gaped, and nothing came out of it. It was common knowledge in the village and beyond that witchcraft was unacceptable. But then, Timina's grandmother was a very religious woman. Nakhumicha could not understand how witchcraft and religion mixed. To her, just like it was in the village, that was equivalent to mixing light and darkness. Timina went on…

"I wanted to scream, but she held my mouth and told me I would die if I did. I was so scared, my friend." Timina said with alarm. "Granny said that Nangekhe, the snake is our friend. She said it would protect us." The semi-scared girl finished her tale with the sound of the bell.

A massive moment of silence settled on their heads for a few seconds. Nakhumicha was scared beyond belief. Her friend, on the other hand, had an alarming calmness on her face. Nakhumicha wondered if she was perfectly okay. *How could she be calm? They had a snake for a pet in their home. Didn't Timina know that her life would be ruined if any of the school pupils found out?* Nakhumicha was suddenly annoyed by her friend's ignorance.

"Does your mother know?" Nakhumicha finally found her voice. She rose to her feet and kept a noticeable distance between herself and her friend.

"No way! She cannot know! Granny said if I tell anyone, the person will die."

"But you just told me? Will I die? I don't want to die!" Nakhumicha's voice trembled.

"You will not die, if you come with me on Sunday to see Nangekhe. I will tell her you are my friend." Timina said, with a lot of confidence.

"Nangekhe is a snake, Timina!" Nakhumicha said, running away, with her heart racing with her. Nakhumicha was very scared. *Why did Timina tell her about the snake? She did not want to die. Granny will be shaken! How could she be friends with a snake?*

Nakhumicha did not want association with a snake in any way. Her life was already complicated with her Malaria saga. Adding a snake to the puzzle meant it made it even harder for Nakhumicha to live. She did not know what to say to Timina when she asked her to come to her house on Sunday, later that evening.

CHAPTER SIX

Even Rats Desert a Sinking Boat…

Timina's grandmother, the Mama Assembly of the Quakers Church, sang loudly. Her voice rose above every sound in the altar, commonly known as "*mazibau*." Only elderly men were allowed to sit on the '*mazibau*'. Every congregate who rose, spoke or shared a testimony was required to address the '*mazibau*' crew with respect and reverence. The crew was made up of men with white, silky beards and slow, croaky voices. Their testimonies sounded like radios running on old batteries, and they went on and on and on when they started playing. They condemned the youth for being immoral and dressing indecently when coming to church. Youths were not allowed to speak or even get closer to the '*mazibau*.' So, the youth separated themselves from the holy crew, staying at the back of the church. They gave the Elders ample time to taste Christ firsthand and count offerings and tithes as well.

The crescendos rose and filled the air as women sang the hymns merrily, men stood still in depression, and youths remained seated at the back of the church, most sleeping off.

Meanwhile, the children were out playing. Timina waited patiently for Nakhumicha to show up. Nakhumicha had promised to sneak out of her church to join Timina on the adventure to see Nangekhe. Timina did not doubt even for a second that her friend would show up. She wanted her friend to see what her grandmother had brought and prove to her that it was harmless. She laughed at the memory of her petrified friend that Friday, when she told her about Nangekhe. Nakhumicha had almost collapsed in fear.

When Nakhumicha finally showed up, Timina was elated. She raised her hands in the air to capture Nakhumicha's attention. Nakhumicha ran to her, and together, they glided down the familiar bushy road. They were at Timina's place in no time. Chicken were strewn all over the compound. Meanwhile, the cows mooed in low, bored Sunday tones, and a black cat sat possessively at the door. Nakhumicha hated cats, especially this particular one. It felt like the cat always gave her a piercing green stare every time she visited her friend's house. Timina fished a tiny key and released warm air from the dark room that stood gaping in front of them. The dark room swallowed Timina and Nakhumicha followed in tow. Nakhumicha's legs were heavy. She was unable to move past the sitting room. Timina came back and dragged her all the way to the inner room. In front of her lay the bedroom of the chairlady of the altar.

It was huge compared to what Nakhumicha shared with her own grandmother. The bed sat at the far end, occupying a larger part of the room. It was neatly spread with no trace of creases. The big white bedcover hung on both sides with two pillows in bright pink pillowcases tenderly sitting near the head. The other half of the room was filled to the brim with boxes, wooden and metallic sitting on each other covered in white pieces of cloth. Next to the boxes stood a wall-to-wall cupboard that went way above them, almost touching the roof. Timina brought her to the attention of a dark brown pot that was sitting alone in a corner.

"Nangekhe, Nangekhe! "Timina called, whistling and singing weird songs. Nakhumicha's heart leapt into her mouth.

Then, the snake's head popped out of the pot, tongue darting, with eyes beady and curious. Nakhumicha allowed a hollow scream to escape her throat. Timina rushed to her and held her mouth. Nakhumicha was shaking. *How could people give a name to a snake and keep one in their house?* The snake was huge. It had shiny beads all over its body. Whenever it slithered on the floor, the beads jingled. Nakhumicha had never seen such a monstrous snake. She thought, *It is going to swallow me.* The snake moved where Timina was and crawled on her lap. Nakhumicha's feet wobbled. She could suddenly not breathe. Watching her friend petting a huge snake made her vision blurry. She retreated slowly, silently praying not to die in that house and be fed to a snake.

"Don't be scared, Micha. She cannot bite. She only protects us from bad people." Timina said, handing her mortified friend the reptile. Nakhumicha, seeing the shiny creature come closer lost grip on her feet and fled, banging on the bedroom door and missing the black cat's tail by a whisker. The chicken flew in different directions when they heard approaching feet, clucking on top of their voices. Timina, without thinking, followed her friend, running after her.

Nakhumicha ran towards the Catholic Church, where her own grandmother was. It was the safest place. Timina, on the other hand, with a snake around her neck, ran towards the Quakers church, thinking Nakhumicha had gone there. The onlookers, seeing a girl flee past them with a huge shiny reptile around her neck, dropped everything they were doing and followed the small snake-bearer. All feet headed towards the Quakers church. Before Timina could undo her mistake, she had revealed her family's secret. Just like that, skeletons were already roaming the village, freed from the closet. The two girls had run in two opposite directions, oblivious that they would never be seeing each other again.

CHAPTER SEVEN

Let Him Who is Without Sin Cast the First Stone...

"Huyu mungu wapendwa, amenitoa mbali sana, afume yeesu..." Mama Assembly started giving her testimony that made all the Quakers envious. Some shouted, "Amen!" in jest while others growled in spite. Not everyone liked Timina's grandmother. She had sat on the chairlady's seat for ages, and all women who grew in faith and spirit were always voted out. Any time anyone stood to oppose her, she would mysteriously step down or just disappear from the church. Women had given up the position and sat heavily on the wooden benches far from the *mazibau,* waiting for her to die so that they could take over.

Being the chairlady of the Quaker Women Association came with lots of desirable privileges. This meant representing the village church in other village assemblies, sitting on the disciplinary committee with the church elders, sitting on the offering and tithes committee, but most importantly, gaining the yearly fund that went to shopping for the Chairlady's house. This left women with bellies full of fat and bile, resentment, and admiration for the Chairlady all mixed up together. They longed for the day that boxes of sugar, cooking grease, groceries, and other goodies would be flowing in their own houses in preparation for Christmas. It was believed that the Chairlady was the mother of all children, so she was given the treat yearly to help her feed the needy children on her doorstep for Christmas. No parent let her child near this particular Chairlady's house, though. She received the offerings from church with glee and relished them with her closest family, her daughter-in-law, and granddaughter. She never bothered making excess meals on Christmas because she was sure no parent would dare let their child come to her home.

"Pwana amekua mwema wapendwa! Amenitenga na muofu. Nimekanyaka nge na nyoka lakini niko bado hai…"

The congregation mumbled 'Amens' here and there as the old woman continued raining praises for Jesus and boasting about what He had done for her.

As the Chairlady went on, spilling tirades about Christ being good to her, Timina struggled through a mob with her granny's snake around her neck. The crowd was closing in on her. They were calling her a witch, murderer, and declaring that she, with the rest of her family should be stoned to death. She felt like a little lamb being pursued by a rabid dog. Timina ran faster, distancing herself with the angry mob that was baying for her blood. She did not need anyone to explain to her that keeping a snake in the house was evil and her grandmother had lied to her about the friendship. Nangekhe was not her friend nor anyone's friend.

People talked about witchcraft in whispers and horror throughout the village and the neighboring ones. Those who were suspected of performing witchcraft were either banished from the villages with all of their property set ablaze or they were stoned to death. It was believed that witches kept totems like cats, snakes, tortoises, and even the hippopotamus for those who live along the great River Nzoia. The witches killed people by casting spells onto them, killed unborn children in their mothers' wombs, caused infants to diarrhea all their way to the grave, cursed men and condemned them to alcoholism, made children fail exams and end up as nobodies in the village and broke up good families. People hid pregnant women from them, washed their children in herbs for protection, watched over their sons during the circumcision period and guarded their homesteads with herbal trees.

Outside, jeers were loud enough to drown the croaky choruses in the Quakers church. Word had spread into the village and beyond, and the crowds were gathering to witness what would be done to the snake keeper. At the wooden door, as soon as Timina ran through it, there was a sudden bedlam. Everyone was on their feet, fear spreading in the building like a bad-smelling miasma. The believers' eyes met the villagers' bloodshot eyes. One group was scrambling to get out as the other was scrambling to get in.

Word, as quickly as it spread, reached the Chief's office too. The village headsman came carrying it, begging, "Please, Chief! Release the police before the villagers do anything horrible to the guilty woman and her innocent grandchild."

When Mama Assembly saw her granddaughter pursued by an angry mob, she sunk on her knees with the syllables of *"afume yesu"* dry on her lips. Timina threw Nangekhe at her grandmother, who caught it in time. There was no time to explain what had happened. The crowd from outside was closing in, and the congregation was in an uproar. The elderly woman was still in an immaculate white gown, white headgear, with a silver cross around her neck, and freshly scrubbed rubber shoes. Meanwhile, she knelt with Nangekhe the snake on her lap. Her eyes rose to the roof of the church in prayer. Would she be saved? The crowd jeered in mockery.

"You have finished me, Timina," the old woman lamented painfully. She motioned the girl to a gaping window and told her, "Run to your mother." Timina did not waste a minute; she disappeared in the bushes after hitting the ground and ran to her mother's salon. No one knew how the pair disappeared from the village, but pregnant whispers came years later heavy with their existence in the city. They never came back to the village.

The church flooded with an unruly mob and a few believers who wanted to witness their Mama Assembly roast in her own fat. Mama Assembly held tightly to Nangekhe as they both started to disappear in a heap of stones. Someone was shouting for petrol, and before the words left the church, *boda boda* riders were siphoning petrol into jerry cans ready to create hell on earth. Only the police siren scattered the mob. If anyone was arrested for stoning the old woman, they knew they would end up in jail. No one wanted to be associated with the near-fatal stoning of Timina's grandmother. Even the haughty-eyed and tongued *boda boda* men ran for their freedom. In no time, the church square was littered with stones and twigs, a few eyes, most hidden behind bushes and the prints of the officer's boots. Timina's grandmother was escorted to the chief's office and later transferred to a police station away from the village. No one ever heard of her again. In the middle of the night, men gathered in groups, broke into her house, carried all they could, and set the home on fire. The village woke up to a flattened grey compound.

It was unbelievable that a whole Mama Assembly, who sat among the chosen few on the *"mazibau,"* was a sorcerer. The news spread across the villages like dry leaves blown by the wind. Every lip spoke of the incident for quite some time. As months went by, then years, grass grew on the older woman's compound, and to date, villagers graze their animals there.

CHAPTER EIGHT

The Best of Friends Must Part

Nakhumicha had never imagined her life without Timina. That afternoon, she sat silently under her favorite tree. She stared at the dark-eyed calf that she had just watered, lying on the grass in the sun, chewing cad innocently. Its tail swished from one side to the other, chasing flies that were determined to land on its back. The calf's wet and stormy eyes disturbed her. They looked like Timina's eyes when she cried. Nakhumicha felt guilt rise in her throat and settle in her gut.

Timina was a short, fat girl with the face of a cat. She was dark like over-brewed black tea. Her legs shot briefly from the hem of her dresses and skirts, fattened at the back and thinned at the ankles like a club. As short and rotund as they were, her legs did not stop her from walking faster than Nakhumicha, always. Timina was so fast and looked like she was on the run always. Her eyes would dart here and there, and teachers always complained of her restlessness in class. Timina fidgeted a lot in her seat. It took a few pinches from Nakhumicha to keep her calm, especially during science lessons.

Nakhumicha, on the other hand, was light. Her skin was smooth and brown, like a properly brewed cup of milk tea. This was the kind of tea that formed a cream layer after settling in a cup for a few minutes. Her hair was dark and coiled. It was rumored that her grandmother came from across the border, explaining their light color. She had big white eyes with long lashes that gracefully flapped whenever she blinked. Her face was long like that of a dog, and her mouth was always sprinkled with a pink petal-like texture. Her grandmother never allowed her to plait her hair, though Nakhumicha really wanted to have her hair plaited. Nakhumicha was slender but curvy and shapely. With her chest already forming out, she looked like a little lady, unlike her friend, who was plump with layers of childish fat.

The two girls, despite their physical differences, were like twins. Their similarities of being raised by women, missing fathers, same school, and similar subject interests drew them closer. They loved each other so much that the other girls in school tried to be friends with each other like Nakhumicha and Timina. Nakhumicha ensured that her friend stayed at the top of the class just like she did. Timina, on the other hand, ensured that her friend's ideas and thoughts were always voiced. Timina talked on her behalf at all times. She also helped her friend with the daily house chores, and over the weekend, she came to Nakhumicha's house to help with the thorough cleaning.

Nakhumicha's heart was in her throat. Her thoughts were in a frenzy. There was a lump that made her throat hurt, spreading the pain to her chest. Guilt turned to anger, and anger turned to fear, followed by an acute attack of sadness. It was hard for her to imagine her friend stoned then burnt to death. It was her fault that she could not help herself from running away from the snake. If only she had been courageous enough to hold it, Timina would be alive. She hated herself for a moment, but then wondered why Timina's grandmother kept the snake. The grandmother was one of the holiest elderly women Nakhumicha had ever met. *It was just a snake*; she tried reasoning with herself, blaming her cowardice. Tears flowed down her face freely, her mouth parted, and she let out a hollow cry, whimpering and shaking violently. The calf sat staring at her, chewing on and on, making her angrier. She wanted to stand up and kick it, but there was no energy left in her limbs after crying so much. She chose to cover her face in her blouse and cried more.

Pieces and bits of her life with Timina came rushing back to her. Nakhumicha remembered going to the river, laughing at fat women struggling to lift water buckets to their heads. She remembered running away from boys and going to the forest to fetch firewood. Timina remembered exchanging words with bullies on their way to and from school and sharing sweet potatoes at the far end of the field. And it all came back whooshing like rainwater down the sloppy village road.

Nakhumicha held her chest, feeling the pain rise up and spread all over her rib cage. Nakhumicha thought she would pass out because it hurt so badly. Her heart was breaking into tiny pieces, and the pieces stuck out, piercing through her fleshy torso. She felt miserable. *How will I survive in school without my best friend?*

"Nakhumicha! Nakhumicha!" her grandmother called.

Nakhumicha sprung on her feet, wiped her tears, and went around the house, pretended to be sweeping the front patch. When Granny called the second time, Nakhumicha ran towards her with a broom in her hands.

"Don't sweep when it's not dusty," Granny blamed.

Nakhumicha sighed with relief. She thought, *I'm glad she didn't ask me why I was crying. Maybe Granny thought it was the dust.*

They had not talked about Timina that day. And Nakhumicha did not want to talk about her.

"Bali Timina kelukha-" Timina managed to escape the fire, Granny said without looking at Nakhumicha. She went on to explain, "Timina ran to her mother's salon, and together they had run off to the city. Her home was lit on fire and destroyed by locals."

Nakhumicha's heart attacked her ribs ferociously. She wanted to smile, then jump in happiness because her best friend had not been harmed.

"Never talk about Timina again," Granny warned. "I don't want trouble with the rest of the village. Remember that I'm a foreign widow staying on a piece of land that's highly coveted. That's enough trouble for me."

"I understand," Nakhumicha said.

Even so, the joy she experienced knowing her friend was safe and not dead gave her energy and the hope of seeing her again someday.

Months went by, and one day, a returnee from the city confirmed that Timina and her mother lived in the city. The returnee informed the village that Timina's mother was now working in a salon in the city, and they were doing well. No one dared ask about the Mama Assembly. Nakhumicha could not help eavesdropping whenever adults talked about her friend's family.

CHAPTER NINE

Pity is a Kin to Love...

Days rushed by, Nakhumicha watched the sun set in the west and waited for it to rise in the east. The nights were bright with the moon and dark with clouds sometimes. She was back in her sleeping corner, on the same mattress, covering herself with the same piece of blanket. Everything was getting smaller except herself. Granny had promised her a new blanket if she got higher than three hundred marks in Kenya Certificate of Primary Education. Nakhumicha read everywhere she went. She read under the tree, on her way to the river, when resting after cutting firewood, and when waiting to pick the watering basins from the cow and calf shelter. Granny had to force her to sleep to conserve the paraffin. When Granny could not afford paraffin because people did not buy her bananas, Nakhumicha would sit in the dark singing science mnemonics. She memorized rivers in social studies and the biblical names in C.R.E.

Nakhumicha decided to stay loyal to Timina. She made no other friends but increased her love for her grandmother. She was the only person who did not leave her. Nakhumicha felt sad, knowing that everybody she cared about left her. Her

Mummy left, her Daddy was a known village bully, her best friend Timina had just left, only Granny stayed. So, she loved her. She prayed for her and did everything her fourteen-year-old hands could do to make her happy. Nakhumicha did them so well that Granny would pause, look at the shinning cooking pots, the cleanly swept patches, the collected litter, water in pots, weeded vegetables, sold bananas, and the smeared floor and she would just shake her head in disbelief and gratitude. Granny loved this girl with all that was left in her wrinkling heart. She took every breath for her. She fed the cows more, added more manure in her banana trees, knowing that she would have to send her to the secondary school of her dreams even if it broke her back.

The older woman and the younger woman now often talked about everything. Granny told her about her early years in the village. Other young women in the village had tried being light like her. Granny confirmed to Nakhumicha that she was from across the border, and her grandfather met her during his peacekeeping mission. He was a soldier. Grandfather had loved her despite the village turning against her. She was the most beautiful woman in the village. Granny confessed with difficulty that those who had hopes of marrying Grandpa hated her. They wanted to kill her. They tried poisoning her water and even sent children with poisoned fruits for her. She survived them all. However, it made the women despise her more. They never accompanied her to the river. Then, Grandpa had to hire someone to bring her water from the dam.

"Your Grandfather paid the butcher so that I could get meat supply three days a week when he was away," Granny said, her eyes moistening and her voice full of nostalgia.

"He was very loving. He loved me so much that he did not want me to have many children." Granny went on, wiping little drops of tears that gathered around her wrinkly eyes.

"Why? Children are good. I want to have many when I grow up!" Nakhumicha piped, handing her granny a piece of cloth to cover her feet.

"Your mother nearly killed me. She tore me like a little monster and came to this world, screaming like a demon set on fire. Your grandfather swore to end the childbearing business." Granny said, getting comfortable by the fire.

"She was a *terrible* baby!" Nakhumicha said, emphasizing terrible.

"Not really, she was a beautiful child. When I got better, I forgot the pain and focused on making my only baby beautiful. I plaited her beautiful hair and coiled cowry shells in it. Your grandfather would show her off to his friends every time he came back from the military camp," Granny said with a smile.

"We spoilt our little girl. She was adorable, but we failed her. Your grandfather died in the war, and when news reached the village, she was torn into pieces. That adorable girl vanished when we buried her father. I sometimes wonder how she is doing. Does she ever think about me? My poor child. If only I could protect her." Her voice trailed off with a tremor.

Such talks left granny emotionally exhausted. Nakhumicha hated it when granny was sad, so she would sometimes change the subject to save the older woman the agony of recalling her long-lost daughter.

"You and grandfather, how did he ask you to marry him? How did he look like?" Nakhumicha chimed in, serving the vegetables, then washing her grandmother's frail hands. She said grace and handed her granny vegetables. Then, she placed Ugali between them. They reached for it together, each pinching a piece. They turned it in their palms skillfully to make little balls. They scooped some vegetables and drop their Ugali balls in their mouths, savoring the hot meal.

"Your grandfather was very handsome. He was the biggest man I had ever seen. The men back home are small with curly hair. He was dark with the toughest hair I had ever touched. He also had a very deep voice. Every time I spoke to him, it felt like I was whispering. He stole me from my home. My parents would never have approved. I had to run away with him. My little brother Omari helped me escape." Granny said with a chuckle, then threw a ball of Ugali in her mouth. She chewed on in slowly and swallowed it with a frail gulp.

Such nights ended with both of them squeezing on Granny's bed. Granny would remind Nakhumicha, "Take care of herself, and never to allow a boy to touch you." That warning nowadays, sent Nakhumicha's thoughts to Dau, a boy in one of the biggest schools in her village.

Dau was the short form of Daudi. Everyone in the village called him Dau, but in school he was known as David. Girls talked about him in excitement and with jolly shrills. Women moved deeper in the bushes when he met them on the road. They asked him questions about his school, looking away from his eyes. They said his eyes had a blaze that could set any heart on fire. He had deep brown eyes with bushy eyebrows and a light moustache above his thick dark upper lip. He rarely spoke to anyone unless spoken to.

Nakhumicha never talked about him. She only thought about him and warmed herself with the thought. She could not even say his name. Every time she sensed his approach while coming from the river, she squeezed herself in the bushes and watched him pass by with the cows and the bulls. She held her breath until his dark, heavily, and firmly muscled feet disappear around the corner. She then stepped on the road and deeply breathed in the air, filled with his cologne. He was the only boy in the village who walked his herd to the river to be watered, smelling clean and fresh.

As Nakhumicha drifted off to sleep, she thought of him walking up the road, from the dam, whistling after his father's herd. Nakhumicha didn't understand why she suddenly thought about him a lot. She wanted the night to rush away so that that morning could come. She wanted to run to school and watch the day swiftly pass by as well so that she could come back home and walk to the river. It scared her, meeting him on the road but she wanted to do it again and again. *What if he doesn't like me? What if my clothes are too ugly?* Nakhumicha was suddenly scared. But sleep stole her away.

The following evening, unlike many other days, Nakhumicha walked to the river after scrubbing her feet and generously greasing them with 'Arimis' milking jelly. She had wanted to request Granny for tiptop petroleum jelly because it smelled better but thought against it. She did not want to bother the old woman. Nakhumicha's heart was warm, and it flapped in its cage with an excitement she could not explain. There was this nudging desire and hope of seeing Dau. Therefore, she walked carefully so as not to get dusty. She was no longer afraid of her chest and her behind, which, though hidden in the almost too baggy dress she wore, had a firm tremble.

Nakhumicha was mindful of the eyes that followed her when she passed by. She had long legs like milk gourds. She was now accustomed to shuffling them gracefully every time she walked down the road to the river. The childish runs and careless splashes were long gone, and the awareness of her exotic beauty had set in. Her smooth hair was now a curly bush waiting to fall on her shoulders. She always walked alone, keeping away from her age mates, who were afraid of the attention she commanded when in their company.

Daudi, on the other hand, was a sturdy young lad. He took care of his father's herd and was in his second year of secondary education. He was the best student in the county when he sat for his primary examination. Every parent wanted their child to be like him. Younger boys admired his demeanor and structure. His arms ran veins that ended in his wide palms like roots of an indigenous tree. His shoulders were wide, giving him a permanent boastful posture. He walked in quick springs, with his heels never touching the ground. Dau was always neat and carried a book everywhere he went. All these details swept many girls off their feet, including Nakhumicha. She could close her eyes and see his details right in front of her. She sometimes shuddered at the thought of her Granny ever finding out what went on in her head.

CHAPTER TEN

Beautiful Girls Break Most Pots...

The best moment of being a village teenage girl was when one walked to the river. At the river, girls would thoroughly be scrubbing their heels on a stone and cover them in a thick layer of tiptop jelly or milking jelly. Some applied soap, especially if it was perfumed, like Rexona or Palmolive. Girls chattered away, sending careless laughter in the air, scaring off birds from trees with their claps. Many boys of their age at that time felt like hiding in the bushes. After all, they were afraid of meeting this battalion of young women who swaggered down the road, swaying their plump behinds, making their skirts swing enticingly with every step they took, intentionally causing flaps of their breasts like a vexed flock of turkeys.

The lone girls like Nakhumicha waited until the battalion was long gone before sneaking on the road with a jerry-can hanging on her back. Her jerry-can was steadied by a piece of cloth tied around her head. As she walked down the road, she hoped that a lonely boy would come up from behind the bushes and walk behind her for two reasons. One, for security, in case a dangerous person came along on the road, especially those known to be using bhang like Wambulwa and Masafu. And secondly, for that warm feeling that a young woman got when she was aware that someone was watching her and planning to talk to her but was also scared. As the girl glided down the road, the boy came from behind the bush with his hands in pockets, walking with a spring. He would likely walk with the girl to the river and wait for her to fill the jerry can and then stroll with her back and drop her somewhere near her home.

That evening, Dau was not on the road. Nakhumicha walked to the river alone and came back panting. She was scared of coming across Wambulwa, so she walked faster than usual, losing the gait she had worked so hard to learn and maintain. Water spilled on her *"kitenge"* blouse, making it sticky and uncomfortable. She tightened her lips in a spiral screw, to avoid gulping down air as she came up the hill from the river depths. She was angry for a reason she could not explain. Then she heard footsteps behind her. She wanted to turn and see who it was, but the scent that filled the air answered her question. There was no need of turning around. Her heart started sprinting in her chest, as her anger melted away, a choking wave of anxiety replaced it. She walked faster, water spilling on her face and down her spine.

"Don't end up like your mother!" Granny's voice danced in her ears, "stay away from boys!" Her words drummed on.

Nakhumicha's heart was now in her mouth. Dau was getting closer. Then he walked past her and stood right in her way. Their eyes met for a few seconds, first hers with anger and his with mischief. But then, the two settled for total admiration and unspoken vows. Dau stretched his big palm to shake her tiny but hard one. Nakhumicha shifted from one foot to the other, praying that no elderly woman who knew her grandmother would pass by and tell her grandmother what she saw. Dau's shake was firm at first, then lingered on for a few seconds then dropped. Nakhumicha's eyes dropped on the road together with her hand. He scanned her face, taking in every detail that sat on it. Dau's hands were back in his pocket. They began walking slowly towards the main road in silence.

"Hello," Dau said.

"Hello," Nakhumicha repeated.

"I've heard of you," Dau said.

"I've heard of you too," Nakhumicha repeated.

With that, Dau looked at her intently, for a long moment. Nakhumicha blushed.

"Which high school do you want to go to when you finish primary education?" Dau's voice sounded like a distant thunder rumble in her ears.

He knew she was in her final year of primary education? Nakhumicha was shocked. She opened her mouth to say "Weledi Girls", but it only came as a whisper. Then, she thought she heard him chuckle. It was a wild dream. Her grandmother would never afford it, but she hoped for a miracle. Something in her heart told her she would go to that school, and she believed that something.

"That is nice. I will come to help you revise tomorrow at your home. Your grandmother asked my mother to have me help you," Dau said, walking slower to fall behind her.

Dau did not give her a chance to respond to his remarks. Could grandma do that? Was he a liar like grandma warned her about? She really doubted if her granny, who found every reason to warn her to stay away from boys, could ask one to come to her house to help her study. That was unbelievable. Nakhumicha wanted to voice her concern, but Dau was already behind her. They had approached the main road, and if anyone saw them together, it would be scandalous for both of them. She silently hoped it was true. She knew the teen code. It meant she was to walk ahead and pretend not to be with him because they were approaching the main road. Nakhumicha felt his eyes on her wet back, jolting her to quicker steps. She wanted to disappear across the bend ahead as fast as she could. Her heart was singing with joy. Dau was coming to help her and it was granny who asked him. She had never been happy.

That night, she slept with a smile on her face. Her mind was filled with him sitting next to her, speaking science with his deep tenor voice. The thought of his thick dark lips saying "Monocotyledon" made her smile. She wanted to prove to him that she would go to Weledi Girls. She wanted him to know that she was also very clever in class and her dream secondary school was not a joke. She suddenly wanted his validation. *When did it start mattering what he thought about me? Who did he think he was?* Chuckling like that when she said she wanted to go to Weledi... He had no right to chuckle.

Weledi Girls was the biggest provincial school in the locality. Every rich man's daughter went to Weledi. Every clever girl dreamt of going there. The green skirts and cream shirts, with brown shoes and white stripped stockings that girls wore in Weledi.... The buildings and the huge gliding gate were a wonder for girls like Nakhumicha. Fear gripped her suddenly. *What if I fail to join the school? What if my granny cannot afford it? What if he already has a girl in Weledi? What if he does not like me? What if he thinks I'm stupid?* Sleep deserted her. Nakhumicha tossed and turned.

CHAPTER ELEVEN

None but the Brave Deserves the Fair...

Nakhumicha and Dau sat side by side under the tree. He explained germination and she was keenly listening. He moved from germination to the human digestive system, to the respiratory system and dwelt there for a long period of time. Then, there were many questions on the reproductive system as well and stammers in the answers. After two hours of science revision, Granny came smiling with a cup of black tea, with the pretense of wanting to know what they were studying. Roast sweet potatoes followed after. Books were kept away and eating commenced.

"Grandmother, thank you for the tea," Dau struggled with his Lubukusu, forcing some pride to it.

"*Karibu papa. Saitia huyu msichana.*" Granny returned with a struggle in *kiswahili*.

Nakhumicha's feet were stuck on the ground, lips on each other, and eyes glued on the dust. When Granny asked her to see her teacher off, she almost fainted. She dragged her feet and followed Dau, who had already said goodbye to her grandmother and promised to come back the following day to discuss mathematics. They walked in silence. Then, just when they were about to go into the main road from Granny's compound, Dau held her hand and stood in front of her. The world stopped in her eyes. There was suddenly no air to breathe. Her heart thumped harder in her breast.

"Come to the river in the evening," he said, making it sound like both a plea and a command.

Nakhumicha nodded like a bobble-head. Her throat was dry; she could not speak.

"I have to go now. I will see you in the evening," Dau said with finality.

With that, he dropped her hand after squeezing it gently and motioned her to go back home. Dau stood there watching her until she disappeared in the bend that led to her grandmother's front door. Hands back in the pockets, he sprung away.

The day dragged by, and Nakhumicha could not wait for the sun to go down so that the other girls could go to the river and come back before she walked down the same road. Her head was full to bursting, pointing with: *What am I going to wear? How will I walk? Is it even safe to meet with him? What if I get pregnant? Is he going to ask me to be his girlfriend? Should I accept? What if Granny finds out? I will be dead meat. I can't go. Maybe I should go. I don't know…*

Her excitement was dulled with the fear of doing the wrong thing. But her heart was beyond her control.

No one had ever asked her to be his girlfriend. Rumor had it that boys feared her because she was very clever in school, and she was beautiful. She once heard girls gossiping about her saying she should wait for the boys from the city to ask her. Some said she would have a boyfriend from college because even the boys in good secondary schools were not courageous enough to ask the beautiful, curly-haired clever girl to be their girlfriend. It was hard knowing how she would react.

Dau, on the other hand, had his hopes high when he saw Nakhumicha melting in his presence. He had never asked any girl to be his girlfriend in the village because most of them asked him first. They sent their smaller sisters with letters and gifts, and he would ignore them. He thought a girl who was brazen enough to ask him out was way too easy. He wanted a challenge, and Nakhumicha was the only girl who had kept all other boys at bay. She was a challenge. When her grandmother talked to his mother about him helping Nakhumicha in her studies, Dau counted his lucky stars. Then he realized that Nakhumicha was also very smart and shy. They had a lot in common. That evening, he swore he would ask her to be his girlfriend.

Frogs were unnecessarily loud that evening, especially the male ones. They croaked in awful tones like they had sensed the competition that the dark, smooth, and handsome Dau was posing. He sat on the edge of the dam, throwing pebbles, breaking the smoothness of the calm surface of the water. Dau watched ripples cover the surface of the dam in fascination. He thought he saw similar ripples in Micha's eyes. She had the most beautiful eyes that were like twin pools of deep water, packed with mystery and intrigue that he wanted to wade inside and explore. His heart left its cage every time she was around. He had spent months watching her walk from the river to her home. He had waited for anyone to mess with her so that he could come to her aid. He had followed her, timed her, blocked her way several times, but he had always been scared of her reaction. Dau loved her silky soft hair. It was dark shiny, and curly. He thought about her pink lips and felt sad. He did not know how to go about that yet, but he swore to learn if she ever accepted him. His heart fled when he heard footsteps.

Dau did not have to turn to know it was her. He had listened to her walk, and he knew exactly how she calculated her steps. The sound of her feet on the sand was like those of *Nasimali*, the milk cow- soft and graceful. Her steps were gentle, moderately swift, and deliberate. She did not throw her legs like many girls in the village who forced their behinds to titillate to attract attention. He wanted to stand up and receive her in his arms, but he thought against it and just sat still. He did not want to scare her. He was an adult, and she was still a child, he had to act like one. He convinced his nerves to stay put by taking secret deep breaths. The closer she drew, the deeper he breathed.

Dau had survived in the village without any scandal. Mothers and fathers were proud of him. Most of his age mates had either been accused of making a girl pregnant and denying it, forcing her to abort, taking alcohol, abusing their parents, peddling bhang for Masafu the bang vendor or worse attempting to sneak girls out of the village for older men in other villages. Dau was known for his good grades, his deep-set eyes, his clean scent and his devotion to his father's herd. He wanted to keep it that way until he laid his eyes on Nakhumicha. Micha was making him break his rules. She was a unique girl. She had conquered the dragon that breathed fire in his body.

"Dau, I have to go back home. It's getting dark," Nakhumicha said then suddenly regretted why she had not just said hi to him.

"I won't keep you here for long. Come sit with me." Dau responded, noticing her fear, impressed by her sense of responsibility.

"Granny said if I sit near a boy, I will get pregnant," the words came rushing out, making her regret again.

Dau wanted to laugh at her innocence but kept it in his heart instead. He wanted to walk her back home and drop his intentions, but there was something about her that sent vibrations of young maturity through his skin.

"You will be standing, Micha. I promise you will not get pregnant." He tried convincing her and walking towards her. She quickly stepped back and shrunk in her baggy skirt and old Ankara blouse.

He saw her clearly under the setting sun. Her eyes were wide with fear but beautiful. The azure color of the setting sun was inside them. Her lips, pink and small, looked like ripe wild peaches.

"Someone will hear us. Come here. I will not eat you. I sat closer to you yesterday, did you get pregnant?" Dau said, trying to hide his impatience.

Nakhumicha felt stupid. Her eyes left his face and settled on the rippling dam. She walked towards him and sat where he was sitting before. Their legs were dangling above the water and their backs on the road. Dau loved that spot. It was his haven of peace on the dam, away from prying eyes of gossiping women. No one came there. Dau loved to sit there, watching the golden ball settling lower in the horizon, conversing softly with the water of the dam, casting the golden rays on its surface, making it look like a spray of gold. The beauty of the dam under the setting sun fascinated him. He never got enough of it. The water obeyed the sun, stayed calm, and let the sun dance with love on it. There were no ripples or waves, just the calm thick layer of gold and a distant green. He would close his eyes and see the beauty of the sun in the dam in Nakhumicha's eyes. She was always calm and peaceful around him. She looked fragile. He longed to have her in his arms just that he did not know what to do next when she reached there. It scared him that he did not know if he read her eyes correctly. They whispered to him. They drew him in; they asked for love.

"I thought you would not come." Dau said, looking in her eyes and reaching out to take her hand. His thick fingers swallowed her lean ones. She did not try pulling it away, so he reached farther with his index finger and touched her wrist. It was delicate and her pulse was steady. She held her breath. The feeling travelled from her wrist through her hand to the rest of her body. It felt like taking a warm shower. Her hand grew warm, and he felt the warmth. He knew he did not have to ask. He knew it was a yes. He looked at her, taking in every bit of her face. She looked like an egg. Spotless, fragile, and very delicate. A sudden urge to protect her gripped him. He suddenly wanted to keep her safe from any harm. He instinctively and silently vowed never to let anything hurt her.

"I want to read you a poem," Dau said, finally forcing himself to look away.

"Is it a subject in secondary school?" she found her voice.

"Ha! It's not. A poem is just like a song," he said, regretting the chuckle that left his lips before he could catch it.

Putting his other hand across her shoulders, he started reading, ignoring the shame and discomfort he caused her. He proceeded to read her 'The Beloved' by Laban Erapu, a renowned poet.

"When I see the beauty on my beloved face, I die…" His voice came sweetly.

Nakhumicha wanted to laugh. It was a weird poem, but it made her feel good. He read to the end without stopping.

"Why is the beauty killing you?" Micha asked, laughing.

He thought she had the most melodious laughter. Her breath was fresh, and her lips parted slightly when she spoke. She was not like other many village girls who laughed with their mouths wide open, with their mouths reeking of guavas.

"Her name is Sandra Nakhumicha," he said, looking in her eyes.

No one had ever called her Sandra since she was a child. She doubted if anyone knew her Christian name. Even her teachers just called her Nakhumicha. Other girls called her Micha, for short. *Sandra* sounded foreign in her ears, but she loved how he said it. He was telling her that he loved her. Her heart was dancing, and there was a permanent smile on her face. He stood up, took her hand and helped her stand up. She gave him one last look, smiled and picked her jerry can and walked to the river to fill it. He waited for her up the road. When he was sure that no one nosy was on the road, Dau came from behind the bushes and fell in step with her. Nakhumicha looked different, holding up the jerry can on her head. Water ran down her face. She felt shy under his stare.

They walked silently for a distance, smiles of contentment plastered on their faces. When they approached the main road, Dau walked behind her as usual. He did not have to tell her goodbye. She knew he would be home the following day and they would meet at the river again and again. She was happy. Very happy. Her evening was bright, and she cooked the vegetables well.

When Granny asked, "Why are you smiling at the fire?" Nakhumicha protested. Granny gave her a knowing look.

"Be careful around that boy Dau. You are no longer a child, my dear," Granny said.

Nakhumicha wanted to say, *I haven't done anything!* But thought against it.

Granny kept speaking. "Although Dau is a good boy, you cannot trust anyone. Especially when you are as beautiful as you are, my girl."

As Granny said *Dau is a good boy*, she had a naughty smile. It seemed to dance alongside the fire around them.

Nakhumicha absorbed everything Granny said but the last bit sunk in slowly. Granny knew Daudi was a good boy. It fascinated her. Nakhumicha promised herself to be very careful around him.

Days flew by. Nakhumicha enjoyed his company during the revision sessions. He held her hand when Granny was not watching. He held her waist when they met at the river and she rested her head on his shoulder while they watched the sun set. The primary education exams came as he had taught her, and she wanted to make him proud. She emerged the best girl in the area- among six primary schools in the village- and was called to her school of choice. Granny sold the bananas, the cow and her calf to take her to school. Her primary school teachers contributed for her shopping and uniform.

On the reporting day, Nakhumicha sunk into her green skirt, tucked in her cream blouse, wore socks for the first time since she was born and dipped her feet in the shiny, brown, leather shoes. Granny, with the help of Mzee Kapanga, the village elder and granny's good friend, walked her to Weledi Girls High School.

CHAPTER TWELVE

Chance Favors the Prepared Mind...

School was a second home to Nakhumicha. Everything about Weledi Girls fascinated her. She would spend the whole day reading novels from the huge library that was always overflowing with books. She mastered her English well and studied the dictionary, the biggest book she had ever seen. The laboratories captivated her as well. She followed all the experiments, volunteered to do some when other girls were scared and drew the attention of her teachers of science. Her long fingers had gathered a little flesh and softened a bit. She handled the pipettes and burettes with the expertise of a scientist.

As the term dug deeper into the calendar, so did her fame in school as the most beautiful form one girl, with the longest hair among the native students. She was also the brightest in English and sciences. Nakhumicha's lack of interest in humanities placed her slightly behind three girls in the whole form one block. Nelly, her deskmate, was one of them. Nelly reminded her of Timina only that she was a bit taller and her skin was the color of a ripe mango. Nelly hailed from the Eastern parts of the country and was in Weledi on a scholarship. She was of the same stock as Sandra, because her school box was always half empty. Their little pocket money and desire to do well in school made them inseparable. Just like she had loved Timina, Sandra came to love Nelly as well.

Together, they studied and talked about everything. Being top girls, they were well known in school among teachers and other students. Being a top fifty student in the school gave you a guarantee of attention from both teachers and fellow students. It meant being considered for all symposia that were organized within and without school. The top three positions attracted awards from various teachers, and she would walk away sometimes with a good sum of money to cater for her termly needs.

Nakhumicha and Nelly stayed blind to the girls who mocked the likes of them, who could not afford the whole supermarket in their boxes, who had no pocket money. On the reporting day, Nakhumicha's Granny had given her fifty shillings, and Mzee Kapanga added her a coin she didn't look at. Nakhumicha never had to use that money. The food served in the dining hall was more than enough for her. Her table was full of girls who had picked her to join them because of her looks. But when they discovered that she had no elegance or refinement, they had started ignoring her. Nakhumicha would serve enough mixture of maize and beans, add a piece of avocado and eat with relish and sit in silence, enjoying every scoop of the spoon, trying to figure out how she failed a sum from the assignments given.

Sandra attended to the duties allocated to her devotedly, swept the floors, cleaned under her bed, and scrubbed the serving pan thoroughly when it was her turn. Sandra also offered to help the classy girls to complete their duties. And in return, they paid her with coins, biscuits, apples, oranges, sugar and cocoa. Some of those things were reaching her tongue for the first time. And she would stare at them, wondering which part of the food she should start biting. Apples captivated her the most. Their smooth, red, and crispy nature, the sweet-sour taste that tickled the tongue and the juice that had no scent at all fascinated her. She had in stock enough bananas and avocadoes picked from her grandmother's farm to supplement her diet during the hard times of the term.

The year spiraled swiftly, and before Sandra could fit properly in her school skirt, form one was lost in a bend. She did very well, received many awards at the end of the year, including the best girl in Languages, two of the sciences, and the most disciplined form one girl. Granny was very elated to see her over the holidays and she worked harder to ensure that she had enough for the following year. Sandra was growing fast as well. Her features were unfolding, and she was blossoming into an extremely beautiful young lady.

Dau was beside himself with joy every day he saw her over the holidays. They continued studying together under the keen eye of her grandmother and stole their way to the river in the evenings. She had grown so fast and firm as well. She talked with the maturity of a young woman with a new intelligence. When the holidays passed, he promised to keep in touch with her through letters. On the day they said goodbye, beneath the sapphire beam of the setting sun, watching their reflections on the calm waters of the dam, he had hugged her tightly and pecked her soft left cheek.

Dau was very proud of her when she managed to get a place in Weledi Girls. He wrote her a letter after a month, surprising her beyond expectations. It was not common for junior girls to receive letters, especially from boys, so when hers came, it escalated her fame in the school. In the letter, he expressed how much he missed her but confirmed that he believed in her intelligence. He wanted her to work hard to get opportunities to go to academic symposiums. Then, she could represent her school in various subject contests.

The first time she went out, they met in one of the big schools in the region. The school was away from home, they did not have to worry about anyone seeing them together. She was so thrilled to see him. There were very many girls and boys present, and each was enthusiastic about meeting the other. It felt perfect. There were no prying eyes in the bushes waiting to report to her grandmother about Dau talking to her. For once, Sandra felt threatened by the many beautiful girls from other schools. She had forced her hair in a tight bun and had her eyes colored with eye pencil for the first time, like most of the girls from her own school, before she stepped out of the bus.

Girls from other schools had their skirts up above their knees; were way too tight. It annoyed her how Dau escorted them with his eyes; a feeling she had never experienced before. Sandra's skirt was baggy like those of her school mates. It was against the school rules to pipe a skirt, and the deputy tore up the skirts of girls who tried piping. She chose to wobble in her baggy one. Beneath that baggy skirt were curves and a behind that shot out from the cave on her back. Sandra's back was naturally arched, making her look like she invited an arm around her waist. Her long fingers had now collected some nails, and they looked like thin pink lit candles.

Dau took her hand after the presentation and walked her towards the school bus. The teachers were still in the staffroom, giving students a chance to socialize before they returned to their schools. He was proud of her. He introduced her as Sandra to his schoolmates. Other girls had also paired up with some of Dau's schoolmates, and boys from other schools and they were slowly gliding towards the school bus.

"You are very beautiful, Sandra," Dau told her, turning to stand in front of her.

Her eyes dropped on the grass that she stood on. He lifted her chin and looked in her eyes.

"I love you with all my heart. I will always love you." He said.

His eyes flickered ablaze. His words burnt her heart and warmed her body. She wanted to fly into his arms, but her feet were spiked on the ground for a moment. Prefects were watching from a distance as well, and any form of misbehavior would have led to her being reported to the teachers. Sandra did not want to join a black book for misbehaving while out. She did not want to be banned from going out. She still needed to see Dau away from the prying eyes of the villagers. Here, nobody knew her or him and if they did, they were busy winning a heart somewhere.

Sandra wanted to say she loved him too, and she was working hard so she could join the same university as him. It was obvious that Dau was destined for success, for he was popularly known in his school as one of the most intelligent boys. He also worked hard to make Sandra proud. That evening, they promised each other to put their studies first, so that together they could have a great future. They also vowed to love each other always. He took her small finger and looked at the long nail. Then, he took it in his mouth. He gently sucked in her finger, sending a warm wave in her body. She shivered with pleasure that she closed her eyes and waited.

"Promise me, Sandra. Promise me that I will be the only one," he growled like a wild animal, speaking with her pinky in his mouth.

"I promise," she whispered.

He slightly bit her on the pinky, sending another massive surge of warmth in her body. Sandra felt like the dam back at home which rippled after she threw a stone in the water. Dau released her hand and pulled her into his arms. He whispered in her ear a goodbye, quickly released her and ran all the way to his school bus. She walked to her bus that was a few meters away and sat in her spot silently.

"I did not know that village girls like you could get good looking boyfriends," Tabby startled her.

Tabby always called her a village girl. Sandra saw no offence in it because she was a village girl and she had no class like the town girls. She only had her brains, her beauty, and Daudi. So, she kept quiet and let Tabby go on. She was not willing to waste the warmth in her heart after talking to Dau on a fit of anger. She smiled at Tabby and looked ahead.

"That boy is in form four. You are in form two. How do you know each other?" Tabby went on.

"From home," Sandra whispered.

"Ooh." Tabby rolled her eyes, "So the village beauty has attracted the village Prince?"

Sandra kept quiet. Tabby was a form four, a disguised bully, and she was not about to give up taunting Sandra. There was something about Tabby that made Sandra remember Masafu. Tabby was known for being rude and mean to junior girls. Tabby's daddy was a permanent secretary in one of the government ministries. She was a rich kid, and some teachers worshipped her. Her father bought luxurious gifts for teachers whenever she did well in their subjects. She had the attention of the whole school in her palm. And being on her offensive side meant trouble for Sandra.

"I think Tabby likes David," Nelly whispered in Sandra's ear when Sandra settled beside her on the bus.

"She doesn't even know him," Sandra tried dismissing Nelly.

"You should have seen how she was looking at him when you guys were walking towards the bus. That girl is hungry for your boy my friend," Nelly whispered more seriously.

Sandra was suddenly scared. *What if Nelly was right?* When Tabby started taunting Sandra Nakhumicha, a child of a runaway mother and a marijuana vendor, raised by a grandmother in the village, the other girls laughed to make the Permanent Secretary's daughter happy. They did not want trouble with Tabby. She would make anyone go on suspension by just mentioning a name to the principal. She was a senior prefect who never hesitated to use her powers to victimize her enemies. So, Sandra twisted her mouth into a tight screw-like shut. She ensured that her anger remained behind her teeth.

"I like that boy. So, you are leaving him for me. Hear me, village girl?" Tabby spilt the venom of every syllable on Sandra's face like a vexed cobra.

The words felt like acid on Sandra's skin. *How could she ask me to leave Dau for her?* Sandra closed her eyes for a few seconds and felt tears well behind the lids. She wanted to let them flow, but she chose not to. Instead, she swallowed hard, forcing the mound that had risen in her throat down her guts. She wanted to grab her neck and pull out the lashing tongue from Tabby's mouth, but she shifted in her seat and sat on her hands.

Teachers were heard, approaching the bus. Tabby walked to her seat and assumed a sweet smile of a senior prefect. Her face was lengthy, with a chin that rounded up too late. Her cheekbones were high, and she had perfect teeth. Since she was a senior girl, she looked like a full-grown woman. She even wore bras in her shirt, which were always showing in her blouse. It was rumored that she seduced male teachers with her bra technique, but nobody dared say it out loud. She was intelligent, among the top ten, with long hair that she held tightly way up at the center of her head. She wore the most expensive perfume in the school compound. Male teachers drowned in her presence while female teachers turned up their noses with disgust and envy.

"Anyone still out?" Mrs. Nanga, the Chemistry teacher, asked.

"Nooooo!" Came the chorus from the girls.

The bus was coughed after short appreciation speeches from other teachers, and a short prayer from the senior prefect, Tabby. Then, the journey back to school started.

"What will you do?" Nelly asked Sandra in a whisper.

Sandra knew exactly what she meant. She just shrugged and looked out of the window, gently twisting her small finger. It was still warm and the patch where Dau bit it was pinkish. It suddenly dawned on her that she was the only one who had promised him about having only him, and he had not promised her the same. The warmth left her heart, replacing it with fear and the chill of the wind that was squeezing through the window made her shudder in her seat.

"You have to leave him for her. She will mess your life, Sandra," Nelly was serious.

CHAPTER THIRTEEN

Fortune Favors the Bold...

"Excuse me, Madam. May I come in?" A lean girl stood at the door. Her wide white eyes were on Ms. Obabu. Her hair was up in a forced bun, making her face stretched. The lean girl stood with her shoulders spread and hands in front of her, folded in a nice, polite gesture. Her school uniform was clean, and her socks had a sparkle in the morning sun. She had come to pick a book from one of Nakhumicha's classmates.

"Come in," Ms. Obabu signaled her, smiling. "I like it when girls are bold and looking neat like this girl. She is just a form one. Some of you are in form three, yet you don't even know how to express yourselves!"

Nakhumicha was lost in thoughts. She did not even see the girl come in. Her reply to Dau's letter was ready and she had managed to rub postage stamps with toothpaste to avoid buying new ones. End term exams were around the corner, and so was the final national examinations for the candidates. Dau was sitting for his final examination, and she wondered where she would get the money to buy him a success card. She thought about Granny, too. Nakhumicha contemplated on using her saved up coins from taking care of the rich girls' chores and assignments but thought against it. She would need that for her transport back home and maybe to buy a few things for her grandmother. She also needed a pair of sandals. The older woman was already sacrificing a lot for her. Granny had sold the two bulls to clear her school fees. Surprising her with a loaf of bread, she knew, would go a long way.

Nakhumicha thought about her mother and felt a lump rise in her throat. *What kind of mother never cared for her child? Did my mother just hate me at birth? What was she doing in the city? Did she have other children? Will she ever come looking for me?* She stopped her tears from flowing when Ms. Obabu, her teacher of Geography, called her name.

"Sandra, what is the difference between folding and faulting?" She barked at her. At once, Sandra knew she was in trouble. Ms. Obabu hated it when students daydreamed during her lessons. She commanded full attention from the beginning of the lesson to the end. Sandra did not like Geography. Most of the physical features that were taught did not make sense to her. She had never seen a mountain, a hill, a lake, let alone an ocean. Comprehending the difference between faulting and folding was just too much. How could the same process form both a mountain and a lake? She wanted to keep the knowledge about God creating the universe with everything in it, commanding their existence. The weak lines and folds forming lakes and mountains did not just add up in her mind.

"Aaaah…. Aaaah…" Sandra stammered, trying to figure out which was which.

"Get out! You are in your own world yet am trying to explain a concept that always appears misses in exams," the teacher bellowed. She motioned her out with a force that shook her entire body.

Sandra walked out of the class with her shoulders drooping. She willingly let her tears flow down the smooth of her cheeks, making her face look like a half-baked chocolate cake with strips of vanilla cream.

"Why are you crying?" Ms. Obabu went on, "I catch you lost in dreamland, staring out of the window like a statue, and now you want to cry?"

Sandra walked out faster, to run away from the teacher's tirade of abuses that was pursuing her. *Why was Ms. Obabu attacking me? If only she knew the weight I carry in my heart, she would not be so cruel to me.* As Sandra knelt outside the door of the classroom, she thought about her granny again. Her heart felt heavy, and she doubled up, holding onto her chest.

Silently, she fervently prayed for her. "Let me find my way home when schools close, please God," she muttered to herself.

The sky was abnormally grey, and the cold air was biting into her face, chewing at her skin hungrily. Her teeth clattered at the approach of the fog that was quickly covering the school. The air was suddenly too thick, and she felt like she couldn't breathe. Clouds sat heavily above her head, threatening to break into pellets. There was a distant cramp in her chest, a kind of pain that just lingered on and went nowhere.

"Young girl, are you okay?" Ms. Obabu asked her after she had finished her lesson.

"No madam, my chest hurts." She gathered all her guts to answer her, startled that the lesson had already come to an end, and Ms. Obabu was already out of class.

"Go see the nurse. If I catch you daydreaming in my class again, I will have you punished." She said with finality leaving, behind a waft of perfume as she walked towards the staffroom. The teacher swayed slowly, perilously balancing her heavy weight on six-inch yellow stilettoes.

"Yes, madam, thank you," Nakhumicha responded, clutching at her chest as she walked towards the school dispensary.

Her chest was in knots, and Granny's face was all over the foggy school. The nurse was not at the sickbay. So, she went behind the room and lay down on the grass, hoping that the pain would go away. She tried closing her eyes, but Granny's face tormented her. She decided to run back to class. On her way back, she spotted an older man coming through the school gate. Nakhumicha thought that she had seen such a form somewhere before. Ignoring the thought, she proceeded to class. No sooner had her behind touched her seat that the watchman arrived and summoned her to the principal's office. Something was definitely not right somewhere.

Mrs. Matumbo sat behind her desk, breathing heavily, eying her through her gigantic eyeglasses that sat on her face like an appendage. She surveyed the girl knocking at the door, removing her shoes and walking steadily towards her desk. The girl's hands were behind her back as they had been trained. Nakhumicha's heart sunk when her eyes met the guest's. It was Mzee Kapanga, the village elder from home. *Why was he here? What happened to my grandmother? Had my mother returned?* For a moment, she wished it was her mother.

"Sit down, young girl." The principal started, politely.

This was bad. Very bad. Mrs. Matumbo never spoke politely to anyone. Most of the time, she would shout in a hoarse voice, her belly gyrating with every word. This was very bad. Why was the older man avoiding her eyes? Nakhumicha sat on the edge of the big couch that students never sat on, then waited. The few seconds elapsed as she waited for someone to say anything. It felt like a whole century. The chime of the large wall clock could be clearly heard from the vast wall it sat on. It sounded like monstrous whispers. The giant clock had the school logo and name encrypted on it. Nakhumicha turned around and stared at it.

"Your grandmother is very ill. You must go home." Mrs. Matumbo said in an abnormally low tone.

Nakhumicha stared at the principal blankly. She did not know what to say.

"*Nakhumicha, kukhuo ali mlukulu,*" the old man started explaining that her granny was in Mulukulu Mission Hospital.

Nakhumicha knew granny was sickly of late, but she was stronger when she left home. Granny had escorted her. She couldn't be very sick. Why was the principal telling her to go home, yet the hospital was just across the fence? Something was not adding up.

"*Kafwile? Afwile arie?*" she addressed the old man, her voice trailing and fading into whispers. There was a sudden lump in her throat, and the pulse in her chest started hammering throughout the rest of her body. Tears blurred her vision, and anger clogged her ears. Hot air shot through her tiny nostrils.

She was asking, "Is my Granny dead? How did she die?"

Why were they lying to me? Rage gripped her throat and shot a hot pain, all over her body. She stood up, staggered towards the door, and passed out before she could reach it.

Nakhumicha gained her consciousness in the guiding and counselling office. Some of her classmates were all over her, trying to sit her up and forcing water in her mouth. The next thirty minutes were blurry and hazy. The guiding and counseling teachers were pounding into her all of the clichés about death, claiming they understood what she felt. They only made her angrier because clearly, no one knew what it felt like losing the only person you cared for. *Did they know my life was over without her?* Nakhumicha wanted them to finish quickly and let her go home to her grandmother. They finally allowed the older man to take the sulking girl home with a promise of attending the funeral and supporting her through it. With a grateful but wary smile, Nakhumicha walked out of the school compound, hating everyone who claimed they knew what she felt.

Do they know that my granny is all she got? How will her education go on? How will I live in our house without my granny? Who will protect me? What happens to me after granny is laid to rest? They have no idea what I feel.

Granny was the first thing she met when they arrived home. She was stretched out in a wooden coffin. They had not bothered putting her in a decent one. It was made of wood offcuts, and they had not gone to the trouble of pulling off the cypress barks before throwing her in it, leave alone painting it. Nakhumicha walked where the older woman lay and fell onto the coffin. She convulsed in pain, choking on her sorrow. She had never imagined this day. Pain ripped her heart open, letting it bleed in the situation. Granny never mentioned that she would die. She promised to be always there. She had said she would be there when she received her degree and became a lawyer.

"*Ufwae kofia ya dikrii kukhu,*" Granny had said when she brought her to weledi. She told her to wear the graduate's hat.

Why did granny die? Why are they lying to me? Do they know that my granny is all I have? My life is all because of granny. I worked hard for her. I labored for her. How can granny just wait until I am in school then die?

Nakhumicha regretted going to boarding school. She thought it was her fault. If she had gone to a day school, she would have seen granny every day and taken good care of her. Nothing would have hurt granny in her presence. Nakhumicha was angry that the older woman was no more. Granny was supposed to wait for her to finish school, get a job, and build her a better house away from the village.

In between weeping bitterly and blaming herself, something on her granny's forehead caught her eyes. It was a bruise hidden behind the white lacy veil that covered her grey face. Granny had no mark on her forehead in life. Where had that one come from? Was it stitched? She scrutinized the old woman's lifeless face and realized there were other tiny bruises on it, neatly concealed behind the veil. It looked like something had hit her. Nakhumicha looked around the compound for the first time in desperation. The faces around her stared back blankly. Something was not adding up. She was strongly convinced that there was more to what met the eye. Her grandmother's home was beaming with the eyes and whispers of men and women. Each one looked like they were about to attack her. Her grandmother's main house was locked, but there was smoke rising from the kitchen.

"Who has the key to the house?" she asked, turning to Mzee Kapanga, who had not left her side since they arrived in the compound.

"I don't know yet. But people are saying it is your father who has it." Mzee Kapanga said in a whisper.

She did not need the rest of the story to know that she was being kicked out of her home. She could see it all in Mzee Kapanga's eyes. The stormy fear behind his whitish eyelashes explained everything on his mind. She understood the old man's fear of the villain Masafu and dropped the subject. No one talked about the misdeeds of Masafu and stayed alive.

She was not going to engage him, either. She scanned her grandmother's body, lying flaccidly in the pieces of wood, one last time. With that, Sandra wiped her tears and moved away from the coffin. She gave her grandmother's compound a desperate examination, held on her school bag, and walked away from everyone. She remembered her grandmother's remarks about the coveted piece of land.

It was hard to believe that someone would go on to kill an old woman just to have her land. Sandra was angry. *I will be a lawyer when I grow up. I hate the injustices widows face in this village. Someone must have attacked grandmother. She was not sick when I left.* A steady flow of thoughts assaulted her.

Without her Granny, she had no home. She was willing to go live on the street but not under the same roof as Masafu. She shuddered at the thought of it. If he thought he would come anywhere near her, he was mistaken. The idea brought tears in her eyes. Everyone in the village knew Masafu. They spoke about him in whispers, and he enjoyed the fear he aroused in people. He walked with his legs widespread, intentionally dragging them in the black tyre-sandals he never removed. Both small girls and boys fled his presence. Small girls ran for their lives with the fear of being dragged into some sugarcane plantation. Meanwhile, small boys ran too; afraid of being forced to ferry bang from one village to the other. Masafu targeted the children of desperate single mothers, widows and rebels, made the children into chain bhang smokers, and used them to peddle it. Some of the boys who fell deep into his trap ended up committing suicide and their parents would not dare condemn Masafu. The area chief stammered every time anyone launched a complaint about him. The local police had arrested him multiple times but later, would release him on bail that he paid with ease. They claimed that there was never evidence enough to convict him every time anyone got him arrested.

Nakhumicha kept asking herself, *how could such a man become my father?* She never knew her mother except from photographs that Granny showed her. She was a beautiful woman with flowing curly ripples on her head. She was shorter with her grandfather's round face, but she had her grandmother's skin color. In the photograph, she was smiling. Her teeth were a neat set, with a sparkling white shooting evenly from pink gums. She was holding a flower in one hand, and the other was resting on her hip. She looked like a village model. That was the only knowledge Nakhumicha had about her mother. She did not look like a girl who would willingly have a child with Masafu unless he was something else then.

Nakhumicha's mother had been sent off the same day she bore her. She had not wanted to see her own baby's face. Nakhumicha pitied herself when she remembered Granny telling her how her mother had wrapped her up, laid her in a corner and left. Though it had been planned, it hurt imagining how it had been, with ants crawling into the piece of cloth that wrapped her. Granny said she had found the baby screeching like a little eagle. She named her Nakhumicha, and when she was baptized after one year, out of sheer luck, the priest called her Sandra just like her mother had wanted. She was, therefore, Sandra Nakhumicha. Granny had told her that her mother never wrote to them when she left. Like smoke, she disappeared into oblivion.

"I have a box your granny asked me to give you. I will give you after the burial tomorrow, but you should be very careful about it." Mzee Kapanga's words caught her just before she left the compound.

CHAPTER FOURTEEN

Death is Doom's Day...

Nakhumicha headed to the dam. This was the only place that still gave her peace. As she sat at her favorite spot letting her feet dangle in the water, her whole life danced in the ripples. She saw Granny struggle to force porridge down her throat. She saw Granny struggle with her on her back taking her to nursery school. She saw Granny plead with teachers to let her stay in school when she did not have twenty shillings for exams. She saw Granny laugh near the fire as she told her stories of her childhood before she came to the village with her grandfather. Nakhumicha saw Granny sleeping uncovered on her bed, tucking Nakhumicha in so that she did not wake up with a cold.

All these things suffocated her. These images chocked and clawed at her. She doubled up and wept bitterly. Nakhumicha wanted to die with her grandmother. She thought about throwing herself into the dam but thought against it. Granny would want her to stay alive and avenge her death. Now more than ever, she wanted to be a lawyer. She wanted to be the one to send Masafu to prison. It was getting chilly and scary. The last women were leaving the water point, so she had to join them back home for her safety.

The compound was crowded with people who were getting ready for the local *matanga dance*. Drunkards who had never stepped in her grandmother's compound now barked from corner to corner, leaking on every bush they set their eyes on. Tents had been pitched and there was music blaring. Nakhumicha had no idea who was funding all this. In the big house, women were oozing in and out. She walked to the door, hoping she could get a chance to change from her school uniform. The outer door was open but the door to her grandmother's bedroom was locked.

"Who has the key to that door?" Nakhumicha raised her voice above the gossip.

The women stopped talking and stared at her. Some were seated on the floor while others sat on the chairs in the arms of some men. They covered themselves with shawls, talking about her grandmother.

"I want the key to this door," she said again, looking at one big woman who had the body of a boss. Nakhumicha had seen her come see grandmother once or twice with a message from the priest or donations from the women of the Legion of Mary.

"*Nakhumicha wamekatasa kuingia huko akii,*" the woman said, avoiding her eyes.

Nakhumicha felt anger and hatred rise in her throat. *Who had authority over my grandmother's house? I know I have no place here, but even Granny has not been laid to rest. Why are these women treating me like a stranger?* She fixed a hard stare on the fat woman and asked with all the force that her throat could manage.

"Shall I bury my grandmother in my school uniform without even taking a shower?" her voice thundered.

"Give her the key. This house is hers." A voice startled them both. The two women turned towards the direction of the sound, one stepping back in respect as the others stood still in awe and wonder.

"You are more beautiful than I imagined, Sandra. Just like your mother when she was your age," the voice went on.

The women in the room sat upright. And those who were clinging on each other tore apart. Their eyes were fixed on the trio. One was a large woman with the key. The next was Nakhumicha. Lastly, was the strange man. The large woman pulled the key from the depths of her cleavage and handed it to Nakhumicha.

"Maybe we can talk from inside," the strange new man's voice went ahead of her as she followed behind, like a sheep about to be slaughtered.

Who is this strange new man? Nakhumicha asked herself several times, trying to recall if Granny talked about her relatives. Granny had once said that she had brothers and sisters and they were all rich and married. They never wanted anything from her because Granny had married a foreigner. But she had one brother, in particular, Omari, and she talked about him with fondness and nostalgia. *Was this the one? Was he the one funding the funeral?*

"I am sure your grandmother told you about me. I am Omari, your youngest grandfather. Your Granny took care of me when I was a baby, before she ran away with that soldier!" Omari's voice changed from a smooth introduction and acquired a noticeably resentful tinge.

He kept going. "She should have married a rich man back at home. Maybe she would be alive now. That soldier stole her and brought her here into this wasteland! I regret helping her ran away. My brothers have never forgiven me to date. But I was young and stupid then. She has died like a beggar. Killed by a criminal! And it is all my fault" Omari was pacing up and down. His voice was shaky. His eyes glittered in distant tears.

The women in the other room were peeping and passing by the door, so he walked to the door and locked it.

"These women are very nosy," he said with a smile then sat on the bed.

Nakhumicha's eyes were still roaming all over him, taking in every inch of his being. Apart from Dau, she had never seen a handsome man like the one sitting on her grandmother's bed. He looked like a sculpture. Omari's face was chiseled long, and his eyes were white and brown. His nose was curved out long and slender with a mouth hiding beneath his moustache and goatee. Omari's voice was a soft, distant rumble of thunder. His hair was dark and in tight curls, shaved on the sides but grown at the top of the head. Omari wore a black suit, with an immaculate white shirt inside. He was very tall, with his shoulders broadened beneath his neck. He looked nothing like a grandfather. On his wrist sat a golden watch that clicked against the golden cufflinks every time he moved his hands.

"I am sorry, I talk too much. I am just angry that these village mongrels killed my sister, and whoever did it will just get away with it!" Omari said, slamming his hand on the small table that was before him.

"Wait until your mother gets wind of this, she will have Masafu, that village goon, arrested and persecuted herself."

Nakhumicha thought it would break into pieces. She shook with the impact of the hit, sending the talking sculpture into a fit of apologies again. She chuckled at how he pronounced the name 'Masafu.' He said it like *dirt*.

What did he mean Granny was killed? Was that why there was a gush on her head? Who could have done that? Why? She wanted to run out and ask who did it, but her eyes could not just leave this sculpture of a new relative who was angrier than she was. She knew something was wrong. Granny could not have just died like that.

Omari rushed to explain. "I am sorry I was not here to receive you when you came from school. The old man, Mzee Kapanga, tells me people are not going to be kind to you, but I will protect you." He said firmly, then took her hands in his.

Omari gave her a scrutiny that looked like a mixture of pity and admiration and disbelief. She felt a wave of peace and calm replace the fear and grief that had weighed heavily on her already broken heart. She felt the pain lift away. She suddenly remembered her grandmother's words one evening when she asked her what would have happened to her if Granny was not around.

The words came back to her clearly: *"Even if I am not here my child. God forbid, there will always be a good person sent from heaven for you. God will send an army of angels from His store to protect you."*

Nakhumicha had lived her whole life, depending on the frail old woman. Her presence was her security. She never remembered the army of angels. Even when Wambulwa filled her with fear on the roads, she knew she would easily tell her grandmother who would in turn, ask Mzee Kapanga to warn the village monster against harassing her, and then it would all be settled. This night, however, sitting on her grandmother's bed, next to a stranger who claimed to be her grandfather, she remembered her grandmother's words. It felt like she had said them to her directly. She suddenly felt safe. A guardian angel had been sent for her, from the store that God kept His army of angels. She looked up for the first time since she knew God existed and thanked Him fervently.

"You just look like your grandmother." Omari's eyes were kind, but a wild nature hid behind his soft brown iris. Nakhumicha wanted to shout a big *Thank you*, but the surprise that was printed on the man's face made her pull herself together in shame. She did not hear a word from the outburst of complements he was showering her with. She just smiled and nodded affirmations and acceptance, even though she had no idea what he was saying.

"Tomorrow after the burial, we shall leave for the city. I can't leave you in this bush. You are coming with me. I bought you a dress and shoes. Hope they fit well. I only imagined how you would look like," he said.

With that, Omari opened the door and left the room in long strides, leaving behind a gust of expensive perfume, quizzical inquisitive eyes, and a confused, happy girl. The women who had gathered around the door to eavesdrop on their conversation dispersed in all directions when the door opened, pretending to be busy around the fire. But Omari, the walking sculpture, walked past them like they did not exist.

Nakhumicha sat on the bed and stared at the women, daring any one of them to try asking her to leave the room. No one dared.

She sat there, watching them coming in for one thing or the other. The cupboard was empty, and the room was different. Most of the boxes that Granny had kept her treasures collected from many years of *Chama* were not there. As they came in and out, Nakhumicha drifted deeper in thought and sunk in deeper into her grandmother's bed. She did not bother closing the door because she knew women would be eager to bring the whole door down to get inside the room. She allowed herself to sleep.

In her sleep, she was falling into a pit, into what looked like an endless abyss. Nakhumicha was turning and turning yet could not see or reach the end. She tried clutching at the bushes that sprouted on the walls of the pit. But when Nakhumicha tried to catch hold of the bushes to save herself, they easily came off. The roots of the bushes turned into big caterpillars that attacked her face with their hairy spikes. She tried screaming, but they filled up her throat, and no sound came out. Nakhumicha turned around and looked up. There was a face, it was Masafu, and he was pushing someone else into the abyss. He was pushing her grandmother. She was screaming for help, and no one was coming to her aid. Granny came tumbling down the abyss, causing Nakhumicha to scream out loudly.

"Sandra! Sandra!" Grandfather Omari was standing by the bed, "You are dreaming? Get up and get ready. The service is about to begin."

The sun rays had snuck into the dimly lit room where Nakhumicha had slept. There was a scent of brewing tea in the room, too. From a distance, she could hear crows calling out on each other in excitement: a sign that an animal had been slaughtered. Nakhumicha wished that she could go back to sleep. She hated the fact that it was her granny's burial day.

Omari turned to leave the room but stopped at the door. He closed the door behind him and whispered to the sweating girl, "We leave immediately after the burial. Walk to my car when you see me leave."

The young, shaken girl, still drowsy in the midst of her dream, nodded in agreement. A curious vexation fretted her. *Where is he taking me? Who will watch over my grandmother's grave? What about the piece of land that many had attempted to grab from my grandmother?* Mzee Kapanga was withering away. He would not be able to stand against the demands of Masafu.

As Nakhumicha walked out of the house that had housed her for sixteen years, for the last time, she left her worries about granny behind. The somber melodies filled the air. Screams rose to the sky. Some women fainted while others staged a wild mourning with screams and stumping of their feet. Men stood still with their hands fixed tightly together at their backs. There was a dark cloud that hung onto the sky, ready to let down a pelting march of huge drops. As the priest summarized his summon for the requiem mass, praising the old woman for being a devoted member of the Legion of Mary, the villagers soured up with impatience. Nakhumicha could see on their faces that they wanted the mass concluded so that they could bury Granny and go eat.

Nakhumicha stood still near the gaping grave, with its grossly red open mouth annoying her. It swallowed Granny's coffin, and the undertakers were ready with spades to cover it with soil. She did not cry. Masafu was among the people who stumped their feet on granny as the soil came higher. He did it with such gist that one would wonder if he did it intentionally so that she did not come out of the grave, ever. Nakhumicha watched him with hatred and bitterness. She could not stand his massive body that bullied everyone at any given opportunity. He must be the person who hit Granny. He was the only person who had the motive to want Granny dead.

A few years ago, Masafu had walked into granny's compound and demanded to have Nakhumicha come stay with his mother, the elderly woman who sold local brew. Nakhumicha was about to sit for her primary final examination. She had cried herself to sleep when Granny told her about the bully's demands. He had claimed that his mother was old and frail as well and needed Nakumicha's help. *Was she not her grandmother as well?* Nakhumicha forced granny to promise never to give her away to the wild family of her father.

Where had they been all that time when she was young? Granny had pleaded with Mzee Kapanga, who managed to pull a few strings from his sons in the city, and Masafu was kept away from the family for a while. He however started claiming that the land Granny stayed on was his because Nakhumicha's grandfather had given it to Nakhumicha. Since he was the father, he claimed the custody of Nakhumicha so that he could access it. The thought made Nakhumicha very angry that she wanted to pounce on him right there, but she restrained herself. Her gown was still new, and it fit her perfectly. She did not want to get it dirty.

Nakhumicha watched the last touches of burying her grandmother with mixed feelings. She was happy that Grandfather Omari had asked her to come to the city with her, but she was also despondent about leaving granny alone in the village. Nakhumicha found a seat next to Mzee Kapanga, who could not stand for long and witness the whole burial procedure. He looked gloomy.

"She was a noble lady. I knew her as a kind woman who did everything possible to protect you," there was a sad tremor in his voice.

"Yes. I will miss her," Nakhumicha said sadly.

"It will be dangerous for you to stay here. Your father will see to it that your life is miserable," he said firmly.

Nakhumicha wanted to shout at him and claim that Masafu was not her father, but she chose to ask one thing instead. Something she wished she never asked. Something that later haunted her for a very long time. Her heart broke at every word in the story that Mzee Kapanga gave. She wanted to know how Masafu became her father.

CHAPTER FIFTEEN

Truth Needs no Color

"Your grandmother never wanted you to find out the truth. She hid it from you, and it killed her," Mzee Kapanga started to let out worms that should have remained canned forever. He let the whole story out, the story of Nakhumicha's mother and Masafu…

When Nakhumicha's mother was about fifteen years old, it had been arranged that she should go back to granny's home, the land of long-nosed and curly-haired Africans. Nakhumicha's grandfather had agreed to it because she wanted the best for his daughter. There, she could get the correct education, go to the best colleges, and even land a better job than what she could have gotten while in the village. She was the only child the couple had, and many people had frowned upon it, especially her great grandparents.

Nakhumicha's grandfather was a rich man. He had kept peace in many countries and had risen to higher ranks in the army. He even led one of the troops of the army who fought the white man's second war in Tanganyika. He had bought land and inherited more from his father because he was one of the favorite sons. At the very least, he was the favorite until he came back home from one of his peacekeeping missions with a long-nosed, curly-haired woman draped on his arm. A woman who could not speak the language of the soil. A woman who preferred colored rice to the local staple food *ugali*. A woman whose fingers were too fragile to even lift a jerry can of water to her head. A woman who could not walk to the forest and fetch firewood. A woman, who could not light a fire in the heart of three stones, sit a pot on it and stir flour in water till it formed a hard substance that filled the bellies of men.

Behind his back, his mother had gone to the pain of arranging a marriage for him because he was always away. A beautiful girl, to the standards of a local son of the land, had been sought after and brought home. She had been fed well and trained by skilled women in the village to make a perfect wife for the soldier. To bear him enough children who he could donate to the army after he had retired. A woman who could go to the river with her sisters-in-law and run along to the forest for firewood. A woman who could step on the stone by the fire and make hard *ugali* for the whole family. She was appalled when the soldier returned home with a slender, shapely woman with a long nose through which perfect Swahili syllables flowed. His parents dropped their faces in shame while the whole village had dropped their jaws in admiration and awe of the beauty that was the soldier's trophy wife. Women gossiped for hours at the river, and men talked about the soldier's fortune in whispers.

When his mother tried to convince him to take the prepared woman for a wife, he threatened to leave the village and never return. The fear of losing a son crept in, and finally, the soldier won the war against his parents for a few years. The village was none of his business. The strange beauty struggled to fit in. She learned the language of the people very fast and tried going to the river but failed miserably on several occasions. The soldier hired someone to bring water and till the ground for her. Masafu was the perfect candidate, for he was big and strong. He did the chores like he was born for them. Nakhumicha's grandmother grew fond of him. She treated him well and fed him the army goodies that the rest of the village only heard of.

When it was declared that she was going to have just one child, her mother-in-law went into a fit again. This time, she made it her business to see to it that the foreign woman left. Another girl was sought again. Tall and slender, just like the soldier loved them. They only failed in painting her light. The soldier was disgusted by her willingness to throw herself at him, yet she knew he had a wife. Nakhumicha's grandmother persuaded him to take her for the sake of having children, but the soldier could not hear a syllable of it. She cried, refused to eat for days, blackmailed him, cajoled, quarreled, begged, and sulked about it to no avail. The soldier, like a rock at the center of a river, defying the hard hits of gushing water and debris, adamantly refused.

Desperate times called for desperate measures. The soldier's mother did what she thought any mother would do for a son in her circumstances. She hatched a plan with the darkness. She knew who she wanted her son to marry. Upon visiting a local doctor in the next village, a love portion was given to be mixed in the soldier's food. The doctor promised the young girl that the soldier would be hers, despite her coal skin by sunset, if she used the portion carefully and as instructed.

That evening, the mother-in-law delegated the heart winning mission to the future daughter-in-law and focused on sealing the fate of the foreign woman. She called Masafu into her house, fed him well, and asked him to do one thing that would lead to Nakhumicha's horrid existence. For the first time, Masafu saw Nakhumicha's mother, the daughter of the foreign woman, and the only child of the soldier in a different light. His mother-in-law fed him again, and he was strong enough to strike.

Nakhumicha's mother, then a fifteen-year-old, was summoned by her grandmother, only to be locked up in the house with Masafu. The rest of the events were gravely horrendous. Nakhumicha could not hear of it anymore. She wanted to go far away from that sickening village. Although the old woman was banished from the village when the act was discovered, Nakhumicha felt like that was not enough punishment. Mzee Kapanga said the horrible woman had later drowned herself in the dam because of loneliness. No one wanted to be associated with her after what she did to her granddaughter.

The story left Nakhumicha's face drained of all the blood and a ghastly flow of the same in her heart. She felt a deep hatred that she had never felt before, for the village that she had called home for her entire life. She wondered if misfortune was generational and if it were, was there a point of redemption?

How could a woman do such a thing to her own grandchild? Having her only grandchild molested just to get to her mother? It did not satisfy Nakhumicha that the old woman had lost her son to the portion that ended up being lethal. The darkness that caused the death of the soldier was gone with the early crack of the sun, never to be seen again. The old woman might have died out of scorn and guilt, but Nakhumicha's heart was burdened by the level of injustice in her village. The defiled girl conceived, and after the child was born, she could not look at it. Nakhumicha's mother could not put

Nakhumicha on her breast. She wanted to strangle it. So, she dropped it off the following day and went off to her maternal home. The foreign land of people with long noses and curly hair.

Nakhumicha felt so sad that she had hated her mother, yet she should have hated herself. She was the product of the hideous act that her great grandmother had planned. She was angry that Granny let her live. She should have died that morning. She deserved the worst treatment. She wanted to say sorry to her mother, but, how could she? Would she want anything to do with her? Did she even know that the man who made her pregnant had killed her mother, and nothing was going to happen to him?

Nakhumicha picked up the small wooden box that granny had left in the custody of Mzee Kapanga and stealthily followed her young grandfather. She never looked back. She did not turn around to see Mzee Kapanga disappear behind bushes. He did not want anyone to pin on him her disappearance. She did not want anything from the village. She wanted to go away and never come back.

As Nakhumicha hopped into Omari's car, she prayed that her grandmother would forgive her for leaving. She also begged Granny to watch over Mzee Kapanga. Nakhumicha did not want any trouble for the old man or her newly acquired guardian angel.

She sat comfortably in the passenger's seat of the black Mercedes, next to her grandfather. For the first time since she was born, she watched the village go past. The trees rushed away, the red road, the bushes and shrubs, the grazing cows, chicken, stray dogs, and mud huts. Nakhumicha gladly let every bit of the village memory rush by with objects on the road. She did not want to remember anything about the damned village that was helpless against criminals who bullied helpless old widows. Grandfather Omari had his eyes fixed on the road. His throat had a funny pulse just below the bulging Adam's apple. She watched it move when he swallowed saliva.

"Your granny took care of me when I was a baby," he started, as if he had seen her staring at him.

"My mother died when she delivered me. My father was an irresponsible drunk. Your grandmother's family adopted me. Your grandmother was the eldest girl, and she nursed me like her own. When she left with the soldier, I was only ten. She tore my heart to pieces. I grew up in their castle-like a son, though." His voice shook with anger. His eyes were moist and red. Nakhumicha was scared. She did not know what to say or how to say it. So, she just listened.

"Then your mother was sent to us. She had just delivered a baby. She was very ill. Your grandmother's letter was written by one of your relatives. It said she had been abused and we should take care of her because her life was in danger back in the village. She also said that her husband had just died," Omari's voice drifted. He could not say anything else. He just drove on. His eyes were intensely emotional. He pulled back the mucus that was almost running out of his slender nose with a deliberately long slurry sound. Nakhumicha wanted to cry.

"Is she in the city?" Nakhumicha found her voice and finally spoke after a long silence.

"Yes," Omari said and switched off from her. She felt shut out, so she leaned back on the seat and stared at the road. *Will I see her? Will I like her? Does she still hate me?* Nakhumicha was suddenly scared. She was a product of the molestation that had probably destroyed her mother's entire life. She suddenly did not want to go to the city anymore.

"Grandfather, please take me back. I don't want to see my mother," she whispered tears brimming in her eyes.

Her grandfather said nothing. He just drove on like she had not said anything. *Is he ignoring me? Is he angry at me as well? Did he trick me into coming so that he could finally get rid of me?* Fear crept into her soul and started chewing at her feet, making them colder as they drew nearer to the city.

"Grandfather, please take me back," she begged once more.

"Young girl, you are lucky that I liked you the moment I set my eyes on you. Or else I would have strangled you myself. If I did not do that back then, then no harm will come upon you wherever I am taking you," he shot back at her.

Nakhumicha was taken aback. She trembled in her seat and held her box tightly. She wanted to open it. She wanted to know what her grandmother wanted her to have before anything terrible happened to her. She gave him one last fearful glance, settled in her seat in resignation, and focused on opening the box.

CHAPTER SIXTEEN

Deem the Best till the Truth Be Tried Out...

"I will ask my son and driver to escort you to school as soon as you are ready," Omari spoke after a while.

Nakhumicha nodded in acceptance and stared at the piece of paper in the box. It was a title deed for her grandmother's piece of land.

"What am I supposed to do with this, Grandfather?" she asked, trying to sound polite, but the shakes in her voice exposed her fear.

Omari looked at the paper then went back to staring at the road. He was a man of few words, Nakhumicha could tell that within the short time they had interacted. She would later discover that he was the kindest person she would ever encounter in her lifetime, keen on details, and gave everything a deep thought before responding or acting upon it. She will grow to admire this trait and even adopt it as well.

"You will have me keep it safe for you, and when you are old enough, you will go back to your village and claim your grandmother's land. It shows that the land belongs to you." He explained, then pressed his lips together in a tight line.

"I don't want it," Nakhumicha said, sucking air in her cheeks.

"You can sell it. But your Granny will be bitter." Omari said after a chuckle.

"That cruel man will kill me before I touch that piece of land," Nakhumicha said, as if talking to herself, then stared outside.

"There is a packet of snacks in that glove compartment. We are not stopping for lunch," Omari said then shut her out again.

Nakhumicha fumbled with the glove compartment till it clicked open and pulled out a packet of crisps and a bottle of Coca-Cola. She munched on the crispy pieces greedily. She had not eaten anything since morning, but she had not felt hungry until now. The crunch in her teeth was deafening and she swallowed the coke noisily. Grandfather Omari looked at her from the corner of his eyes and smiled. He liked her. She had her mother's eyes and smile. He did not know how to go about it, but he was sure, Zari would love her even if it took ages.

Omari remembered with both fondness and bitterness how he came to be with Zari. Zari was between a little girl and a young woman when Omari met her. She was very fragile and weak from the journey she had made from her village to the city and the illness that was nibbling at her body. Her wide eyes were always full of fear, and she was very edgy. When she arrived in the city, Omari had been scared she might die. His parents were ancient, and his brothers had at first refused to take her in. They had called her a *kafiri*. Omari had done his best to convince his brothers that she was the daughter of their only sister even if she deserted them. Even if their mother had chosen the hard-haired soldier over their close cousin whom they had wanted her to marry. Omari explained that she had regretted it; that's why she sent her daughter to them.

"But she is not a pure breed. Who will want her? What will we do with her? Do you think that thing can replace our sister?" Ahmed, the eldest brother, had asked, bile dripping on his twisted lips, his face in tight knots.

"I will have her," Omari had quickly said, wishing he could take back the words.

She was a Christian, had just given birth, and left a baby behind. She had no idea what being a wife meant. She was only fifteen very ill, scared, and deeply traumatized. She had hoped for a warm reception from her uncles, but they had all treated her like an abomination. She hated her life, but a streak of light in Omari's eyes, her youngest uncle, brought a flicker of hope in her otherwise complicated situation. Zari somehow felt that he wouldn't let her die.

"What do you mean you will have her? She is a half breed, you fool!" Ahmed spat red saliva on the ground, a mixture of herbs and cinnamon.

He loved chewing on cinnamon sticks. Omari wanted to shoot back at him, but he knew it would only make him worse. He was the administrator of their family legacy, and their father was dying. Therefore, he could not intervene. Ahmed was like the second dad to Omari. He had to respect him if he wanted a share in the inheritance. Being adopted, he knew any mistake would lead to him being disinherited. Even though this family had never treated him as an outsider, he knew he had no right to anything. By taking in Zari, he was pushing his luck beyond limits. Going against Ahmed was like committing financial suicide. Omari also believed in the healing poultices of time, even on the deepest wounds.

"She is our sister's only child. Think about it, Big Brother. Think about Zaitun. You loved her once. She is still our sister, even if you hate her now…" Omari pleaded with his brother. "You cannot hate her in her death too, brother."

Ahmed's face was hidden in the dyed beard that spared only his mouth, nose, and eyes. He looked like an angry chimpanzee. His eyes were dangerously red. It was clear that when Zaitun, Nakhumicha's grandmother, eloped with the soldier from rural Kenya, he was astounded. He shapeshifted from a kind, respectable, neat man into a bushy hostile chimpanzee that would pounce on any creature that dared stand in his way. Ahmed was the most hit as Zaitun was betrothed to his best friend and a cousin of the family, Abdul. It was a shame since he had even negotiated for her and gotten the best price on her. He had ensured that Abdul would make her happy because she was the only sister they had. Ahmed had even demanded that Abdul built a castle for his sister as her wedding gift, and the man, being very in love and eager to please his in-laws, had obliged without argument. It was going to be the biggest surprise ever heard of in the territory.

Ahmed did not leave the mosque for a whole week. He did not eat, bathe, or talk to anyone for days. He also started growing a beard. The family settled the debt left behind by the runaway bride, lived through the shame, and moved on, but Ahmed never moved on. He loved his sister with all he had in him, and when she left with the soldier, she left with a part of him that was never restored.

"That woman ceased to exist for me when she chose the soldier over us. She is no sister of mine," Ahmed shot the words on Omari's face like one would pepper spray on an enemy.

Omari knew he had to shut up at that point. He bowed to his brother in respect and walked to his unfinished castle, heartbroken. Zari was the only memory he had left of his loving sister Zaitun. He thought about the songs Zari sang for him when he was a small boy. He remembered her happy, docile face, her tender touch, and how she held him on her freshly blossoming bosom. The warmth of her smile and the worry she always had when he went missing in town. He remembered her hennaed feet running through the town to find him. She saved him from the wrath of his elder brothers every time.

The wind was ghastly that evening, and the chill ate into his skin. His heart was throbbing in anger and sorrow. How could he turn down the girl? How could he look in her deeply wounded eyes and say she was not accepted in their home? Omari ignored the wind and the sand that attacked his face. He ignored the greetings of his neighbors and the smiles of virgins who hoped to melt his heart. It was known all over that he was searching for a well-bred virgin to marry. And since his family was known for its wealth and influence on political matters in the territory, getting one was going be a walk in the park. He had no eye for any, though. It was like he was waiting for something different. Something that was not the obedient virgins of the town raised in a castle, and taught nothing else but making themselves beautiful, rolling the waist, and cooing at their husband's calls.

Omari hated their simplicity. He loved their respect and submissiveness, but he wanted something fierce. He wanted someone with a brain that was not covered in the burqa. He wanted a woman who would look him in the eye and defy him when necessary. He hated to spend the rest of his life with someone who had no voice. Every man wanted a pretty face, with good blood and skills in various things, but that was not enough for Omari. It lacked pepper in it. He approached the gates of his castle and ignored the watchman who greeted him with a smile.

Omari strode towards his compound in silence. A pensive dreamy look sat possessively on his face. He did not notice his maid smiling shyly at him. He broke into an urgent run upstairs and softly knocked on the door where Zari slept. He hoped he would find her healed. The family doctor had said she would get better if she got lots of fresh air and had someone talk to her. True to his thoughts, Zari was seated on the bed, looking out through the window. Her back was straight without any feminine arc. There was a faint scent of soap in the room. Her hair flowed down her back. It was jet-black with a Nubian thickness. She heard him approach, but she did not turn around to confirm it. Years later, she will be receiving him in the same room, the same way. With her hair flowing into the arc of her back, well-formed and fully matured, eyes fixed on the view of the city.

"I enjoy watching the city too." He tried getting her attention.

"Mm... Okay, you grew up here," she blabbered, making her first impression on him.

"How are you feeling today?" he asked, smiling at her back.

"I miss my mum. Will I ever see her again?" she asked. Her voice was so sad that it stung his heart. She was crying. Her eyes glittered with tears and sadness.

"I don't think so. She is not allowed to set foot here." Omari replied. He immediately regretted his bluntness.

Zari turned to look at him. For the first time since she arrived, he saw her standing straight. She was tall. Her body was slightly heavy with excess flesh, but he attributed it to baby fat. Her chest moved up and down rhythmically. She was not shy. She looked in his eyes. He noticed that they were deep and piercing. The tears had made them wet and slightly swollen. The twinkle was hidden behind the cloud of sadness, but he knew, they would be shining brighter soon. She was a beauty to behold, even in sadness. Omari's mouth opened to say something, but his throat was suddenly parched, and the words piled on each other in his gut running out in an incomprehensible stampede. He was suddenly afraid of saying the wrong thing to her. She slightly chuckled at his abrupt stammering attack.

"Help me go back to school. I want to finish my studies and be a lawyer." She said, looking straight in his eyes. It sounded like an order.

Omari was taken aback by that demand. All girls wanted to have a rich man marry them so that they could get the security of a beautiful home. They did not take education seriously. Men also ensured that most girls didn't attain academic excellence. Immediately when they blossomed, they were betrothed. If the husband wished for his wife to continue with her studies, she would be allowed but most preferred them sitting at home, dolling up and looking pretty. Zari was a different girl. From that moment, he knew he had landed the right girl. He stopped worrying about Ahmed and decided he would take her to school when she got better and see her through college, then marry her.

"I will pay for your school on one condition," he said to her, avoiding her eyes.

"You don't have to if you have conditions," she shot back.

"What?!" he was dazed.

"You are my uncle, you should love me enough, and why do you want to fix conditions on helping me?" she asked, fully facing him. Her voice was calm but stern. Omari wanted her to go on. Zari had the sweetest voice, firm and thick, yet smooth like fresh banana juice, densely flowing. She was already a lawyer and did not need to go to school to be one. She had him pinned against the wall.

"Okay. I will help you." He said and forced himself out of the room. She was a spoilt child; he thought to himself. She must have gotten her way always. She actually knew what she wanted and did not hesitate to go for it.

The following weeks and months were the hardest of his life. Omari had to convince Ahmed to allow him to help Zari. Even so, going past his beard was harder than going through a bamboo forest at night. Ahmed screamed at him, threatened him, brought in the other brothers and neighbors to help talk to Omari, but he stuck with his decision.

"Why are you marrying this girl?" Ahmed had asked.

"I love her," Omari answered in the simplest way possible.

It was a stupid answer. He was lucky that culture would allow him to marry her since she was a half –breed and Omar himself was not a blood brother to Zaitun. Not many men married for love. If it were so, anyone would marry anything. Men married for class, for social compatibility, for contracts, for a favor, for positions, because they had been forced by their parents, for wealth, for purity in lineage and many other reasons but not love. Ahmed knew nothing about love for a woman. He only knew his rights over her, the comfort of having someone labor for him through the day and dance to his tunes through the night.

"I have invested in you, Omari. You are like my son. Please don't do this." He begged for the first time after the growling and roaring failed.

"You are right Ahmed; I have never disrespected you. Since you took me in, I have grown up knowing you as my father. I beg you this time because it is the right thing to do. Allow me to do this one thing my way, please. I am a grown man now, Ahmed." Omari tried his luck once more.

"You will kill dad with this decision. You are a bad omen in this family," he said with finality, fishing a cinnamon stick and biting it angrily.

"Mum would be okay with it if she were alive. She would think Zari is an intelligent girl. She would understand that I did it for our sister," Omari's voice was full of determination.

"What about dad?" Ahmed asked, turning to him suddenly.

"We don't have to tell him. He has had enough trouble with his illness," Omari said, avoiding his brother's eyes.

Ahmed did not say anything to Omari for the next one month. Zari, on the other hand, did her best. She quickly enrolled in Muslim classes and excelled in Arabic. She got high scores in secondary school and was admitted to law school. She was focused. Omari watched her transform from a traumatized young girl to a beautiful, extremely unique, confident lady. She had a neatly curved waist, and the blend in her genes gave her a slightly voluminous bottom. Her walk was always graceful. She was painfully shy and afraid of male company. Even so, she was focused and goal-oriented at the same time. Soon, her other uncles and cousins would start noticing her and throwing greetings at her. She returned them with the expected humility of an impure breed, hidden in the confidence of a learned woman. Ahmed bought her a saree one of the holidays. He smiled at her often with time. A few years later, Ahmed would shave his beard, put on a tuxedo, and walk her down the aisle, handing her over to Omari. He would be smiling all the way.

Omari watched her with satisfaction, proud of what she was becoming. He trusted his instincts when they affirmed that she would finish school and come back to him, even when his brothers and cousins thought otherwise. So, he waited.

When he made his intentions clear to her five years later, she smiled and dropped her eyes on her long-intertwined fingers. She had just turned twenty-one and was headed towards completing her bachelor's degree in law.

"I thought you would never ask. I know you are making a huge sacrifice for me. I promise I will never let you down," she had said, with her eyes moistening.

"I think Ahmed will let me marry you because I am not a blood child in the family. I still owe them, though." He had said, gathering her in his arms to seal a promise of love.

Omari had visited her in college and taken her to one of the most expensive hotels in the city for dinner. Zari had grown used to his abrupt visits, and she waited for him anxiously sometimes, checking the parking lot. She was one of the few women from the territory whose relatives or suitors allowed to pursue education.

Omari's heart flew to her, and for the first time, he gathered her in his arms. It felt perfect. Zari did not feel a rush of fear all over her like she did when her male college-mates hugged her. Omari was gentle and kind. He did not squeeze her like a pervert. He just held her and listened to her heartbeat behind her burqa. She wore one every once in a while, in college, but Omari liked it better when she didn't. He loved showing her off to his friends. Her legs were fleshy and perfectly chiseled. They were long. She also had chubby arms. She was different from the skinny local girls that his elder brother referred to as pure breeds. Omari loved this mixture of distance and local in Zari. He had toyed with the idea of marrying a girl who was not from his territory, but the fear of rejection and fights with his elder brother made him give it up.

After Zari had cleared her studies, he helped her secure a job in the local courts, amidst the sneers of other women who wished they had her life and the frowns of all men who thought the place of women was nowhere beyond their husband's homes. Zari knew how to work around it. Her firmness, expertise, and gentleness in handling clients and lords of the bench earned her quick promotions. No one challenged her intelligence, which was discreetly coated in her meek nature. Men realized that her presence was neither a competition nor a threat. They dropped their guards around her and treated her with respect, especially since they knew Omari as well.

When Zari was finally married to Omari, her life took a different dimension. She became a mother so fast that she decided to focus her energy on raising her family. Omari loved her and supported all her decisions. He loved her more when she bore him two sons in five years. Zari had wanted a baby girl, but when she tried for the third time and bore a son again, Omari put a stop to it. She started her own law firm after the birth of Hussein, Hassan, and OJ-Omari Junior.

"I have to go somewhere far for three days, love. I will be back with a guest," Omari had told his wife when the news of his sister's death reached him.

Ahmed had warned him against going to the village where her sister was married, but he chose to go anyway. Her sister had mentioned in one of her letters that Zari's daughter had grown big. He wanted to bring her to his wife. He wanted his sons to have a sister. Omari also wanted his sister to have a decent burial, and he was sure no one would give her that in the village. It was hard to tell how Zari would react when she saw her daughter, the baby who was conceived as a result of pain and betrayal. As he drove to the village, he relied on the directions in the old letters. He prayed that the girl looked nothing like the father. If she had little Arab in her blood, she would blend well in the city, so he crossed his fingers.

CHAPTER SEVENTEEN

Earth Has No Sorrow That Heaven Cannot Heal...

Nakhumicha's eyes stayed on the road. Her radiant face was pale and dreamy. Her life in the city flashed in front of her through a fantasy. She ate food that was not filled with maize cob fire smoke. Her rough, cracked heels walked on the woolen mats. There were way many vehicles going to places in numbered buses. And there was electricity that allowed people to walk and work day and night. It was a life she never dreamt of. The life she only read about in novels and heard of in stories of girls from big towns in her school was finally beckoning her. Nakhumicha thought of how her schoolmates would react if she came back to school, after the funeral, in a sleek car. The black Mercedes, slithering on the gravel of the school's car park, played in her head. Nakhumicha saw herself alight from the car, ensuring everyone who cared to peep through the classroom windows saw her, with an expensive new school bag on her back, a new uniform, with her blow-dried hair tight in a black band, her long legs crowned in new shoes and socks and her grandfather's driver carrying her shopping to the secretaries' lounge to be inspected.

Nakhumicha imagined the plump selectively snobbish secretary run to greet her and politely tell her, "Sit on the waiting benches," as her shopping got checked. She saw her flip through the papers, assuming that wealthy students didn't carry illegals to school like the poor students. It amazed her how those secretaries assumed that rich girls carried no illegals, yet they brought juices, alcoholic drinks and funny chewing gums to school with them. The poor girls were denied a chance to have their avocadoes and bananas in school due to the claim that peelings littered the compound. Her dreamy smile vanished at the thought of how she had been treated unfairly just because her grandmother could not afford to bribe secretaries to favor her.

"Why are you so distant, Sandra?" her grandfather asked her.

"I thought you did not want to talk," she said, shrugging. *What a barefaced girl!* He thought.

She reminded him of Zari. Sandra had her nerves and resilience. She had just lost her guardian, yet she talked like she had already moved on, just like her mother did when she came to the city. Zari had left behind a baby, suffered a brutal molestation, and yet she just moved on like nothing had happened. Zari had never spoken about her child. She never talked about her mother or dad. She just moved on, had her career blossom, with the roses in her marriage forever watered, and the thorns carefully clipped. Zari took care of the four men in her life devotedly. And here he was, carrying a daughter she had abandoned sixteen years ago, taking her back to Zari. He was going to re-unite the two ladies and was willing to go through any hurdle that would stand in the way of the reunion.

"Why didn't you want to come with me, suddenly?" he asked when he remembered Sandra's frightened face a few minutes into the journey.

"If I am going to meet my mother, I don't think she wants me. I will cause her the pain that she has probably worked so hard to forget. I would rather suffer in my dad's hands." Nakhumicha said, her voice trailing in a tremor towards the end.

He knew she was about to cry, and he was not ready to deal with a crying girl at that time. So, he changed the subject.

"My sons will be happy to see you." He said, quickly.

"Ooh, how many are they?" she asked.

"Three. Hassan is the eldest, in form one, Hussein in class seven, and OJ is in class four," he said proudly.

"Ooh. No daughters?" she asked.

"No daughters. But you can be one if you want to," he said, touching her shoulder.

"What about your wife?" she asked, intentionally saying the words very first.

"Let's find out," Omari said, turning in on a narrower road.

She had expected to see the city in the dark. Omari explained that the city was some distance away from residential areas. Her heart thumped against her chest. His heart was racing too. She could see it through his throat.

"You did not tell your wife I was coming?" she tried again.

"We are here." He said, hooting loudly, deliberately refusing to answer the question.

The house behind the rolling gate knocked the wind out of her lungs. It was huge and majestic, set apart from the rest of the castles that seemed to have the same structure and design. The gigantic house was made of white, green marble and glass. Right next to them, bulbs filled with green, red, and orange helium shined brightly, casting a rainbow of rays on the manicured lawns, trophy trees and the granite pavements. The watchman was a small man with tiny limbs that exaggerated his agility. He closed the gate very first and followed the pulling in the car in quick steps. When Omari came down, the watchman was already working on the boot carrying the luggage towards the big house. Lights were switched off in most of the rooms, but one had the lights on, and the window was open.

Omari was looking at the window, so Sandra followed the gaze. There was a form seated, looking out. Sandra could tell it was a woman, and the expression on Omari's face told her it was his wife. She was a neat shadow.

"Welcome home, Sandra," Omari said and started hopping up the few front door flight of stairs like a giant grasshopper. Nakhumicha followed in tow, noticing that he only called her Sandra. So, she made up her mind that she would be Sandra as long she remained here. The nimble watchman was ringing the doorbell, and on the second ring, a short woman with fat hands and legs opened the door. The short woman's baggy dress was forced in place by the apron that she wore around her global waist.

"This is Munaa. She is our house help," Omari introduced the small-toothed grinning woman. Munaa's teeth were widely spread in her mouth and they looked like they were barely stuck in her pink gums.

"This is Sandra. She will be living here. Make a room ready for her." With that, he walked into the warm living room.

Munaa had a sudden frown on her oily face. She picked Omari's bags and started going upstairs. Sandra was fixated on the ground. She was not sure if she should take off her shoes or walk on the woolen mat in them. The grey woolen mat ran from corner to corner, under the huge fluffy grey and white couches that had brightly colored pillows strewn all over them. On the wall were paintings in golden frames and writings in Arabic. There were stars and a moon on one of the paintings. The other wall was a collage of family photos. Sandra had to move closer to see them, so she decided she had a lifetime to do so if she was going to live there. Then, she left them alone in the meantime. Instead, she explored with her eyes. The other wall had a wall unit that started in one corner and went all the way to the other. There was an array of glasses, china, cutlery, glasses, bottles of wine and scotch. A huge screen was fitted in the huge hollow on the unit, and beneath it was a neat assortment of books. Next to the television stood speakers, long and tube-like, and soft music breathed from them.

The sound of approaching feet attracted her attention to a spiral staircase that she had not noticed. Delicate, slender feet in pink slip-on shoes, the woman slowly descended down the stairs. Purplish polished toenails shined bright in the light that gave the room a heavenly luster. Sandra waited for the whole body to glide down the stairs; her eyes glued in the direction. Omari was standing at the center of the living room. He watched his wife sashay down the stairs in admiration. She was in a sleeping gown, and her hair was flowing on her back. He had intentionally waited for her downstairs because he had a surprise for her. He wanted her to meet the girl tonight and decide whether she wanted her or not. If she did not want her, he would have her stay in school even during the holidays and maybe ask one of his friends to take her.

Zari cavorted towards the pair, enjoying the dazing effect she had on them, leaving behind a waft of a sweet-smelling cocktail of scents. Sandra could not take her eyes off her. She looked like an angel. Omari swallowed her into his hairy arms and planted a hungry kiss on her pink lips. He then stepped back and held her at an arms-length distance, taking in every fiber of her being. It was almost twenty years now, and she seemed new and exotic every minute, in his eyes.

"You are beautiful," he whispered.

"I know, honey. I missed you. How was the burial?" she poured the fresh banana juice from her mouth.

Omari was so shocked! How did she know?

"You can't hide anything from me Oma, I know you so well," she said, reading his mind.

"I am sorry, love. I just did not want to make you sad," he explained.

"It's okay. My mother had suffered enough in that village. Let her rest in peace." Zari was her usual self. Nothing brought a quiver in her knees. Not even the death of her own mother. She was always strong and level. Omari admired her strength a lot.

"Where is my daughter?" she said, walking towards Sandra.

Sandra's vision was fuzzy. Her eyes were surging up, and she struggled to hold her tears. She had been watching them love each other, and she could not help it. Her mother was the prettiest thing she had ever seen. She looked like a full moon in a clear sky. Her walk was graceful and calculated. Her hands were very soft, velvet soft. She reached out and touched Sandra's face.

"Ooh, my girl! I thought I would never see you again. You are as beautiful as I had imagined you." She said softly.

Her eyes had tears too and Sandra was afraid if she wiped them off with her own fingers, she would cut her silky face with her hard-beaten hands.

Sandra just stood and waited. She did not know what to say. Sandra had spent most of her life struggling not to be like her mother. Granny had never specified what her mother did, but she was sure it was something bad. She had created images of a woman who was cruel and uncaring in her head. She had spent most of her energy hating her. Now she stood before the woman she never wanted to meet until just a few days ago. And Zari was nothing like she had imagined. She did not know what to say to her because she only had terrible things to say.

"You don't have to say anything, my love. I don't know what your grandmother called you. But I wanted to call you Sandra," Zari went on, "I never forgot your face. I only saw you once before I left, but I have carried that image for the rest of my life."

Zari was choking on her words. Omari had never seen her like this. It broke his heart. He wanted to go to her. He wanted to tell her she had done the right thing coming over to him and leaving the baby behind. A baby would have been an obstacle. She would never have gone back to school. His family would not have let her marry him. It would have been harder than it already was. However, he chose to give the mummy and daughter space. He just let them cuddle and hug and cry and cuddle again and talk, then cry and cuddle again through the night.

Sandra told her mum about her grandmother, the village, and how she had grown up. Her mother just stared at her, cried, held her, admired her, and held her again, tighter by every passing second. Sandra had never felt so emotional. She had never been happy. Food tasted better. Munaa had served them before she went to bed. By the time the two were going to bed, it was way past midnight. Omari had promised to let the driver and one of his brothers to drive her to school when she was ready. The boys were on recess since they went to an international school. Sandra wondered what it would be like meeting them the following day. Would they look down upon her? Would they let her share their parents? Would they be kind? Even though she had gone through the hardest part with her mother, there was a distant worry about her difference from the rest of the family. It would be hard in the future, to blend in completely.

That night, Sandra had slept in her own bed, spread in pink and white. She had a whole room, a bathroom, and a dressing space. It was like a dream. She wanted to scream and tell the world, that she had finally found her mother. She wanted to go back to primary school and tell her classmates about her mother. Her grandmother's box was still in her hands. Sandra opened it one more time, took out the title deed and the picture of her grandmother that she had carried. She pinned the picture to her bed and kept the paper inside her closet.

Sandra promised Granny, "I'll get you justice one day." Then she sighed and looked up. "Granny, I wish I could tell you about my mummy. You were wrong in thinking that mummy was bad." She then sunk in her comfortable bed after a long, warm shower and drifted to sleep.

"What will Ahmed say? My daughter is here with us, Omari. What if they don't accept her?" Zari asked when she finally walked out of the bathroom.

"He is too old for a fight now. Besides, we are all grown and can decide who to invite in our house or not to. By now Ahmed knows he cannot decide for me. I don't want to think about it, darling. I am happy that she is here. I love her. Her brothers will love her too. She is an amazing girl. That's all that matters," Omari, who was almost drifting to sleep, said sitting up in bed.

"But, darling…"

"No 'buts' sweetheart. All I want to do right now is hold you in my arms. I have missed you; you know?"

"Promise me. You will protect her," Zari begged.

"I promise," Omari said, reaching out to her.

CHAPTER EIGHTEEN

Even a Full Moon Cannot Block Stars from Shining...

The following day, Zari invited her in-laws and friends to dinner. She was going to throw a huge feast to introduce and welcome Sandra. She was beside herself with joy, instructing servants here and there. There was plenty of spiced rice, coated meat, chicken, fried fruits, raisins, and sweet dates. The house smelt of food and fruits.

Sandra and the boys were already bonding in the garden, and Zari watched them through the window. The boys were listening keenly to something Sandra was saying. Her heart filled with bubbles of joy. Her pink lips spread into a sad smile. For the first time, the fear of meeting her daughter and even holding her in her arms was lifted. The memory of how she got Sandra was now at the back of her mind, and it felt like a distant throb. Zari thought about her mother and silently thanked her for raising Sandra. She felt tears well up in her eyes, imagining how her own mother had struggled alone in the village after she left. She thought about the cruelty she must have encountered. She remembered how she had asked her never to look back when she left the village.

"Don't even write to me. The letters will break my heart. I know my brothers will be cruel to you, but I am sure Omari will take good care of you," Granny had said, crying. Mother and child had held on each other tightly for the last time before she stepped in Mzee Kapanga's friend's pick-up truck. With that, strange man had taken her all the way to her mother's place and dropped her at the gate.

"They are already bonding," Omari's voice startled Zari. She came back from her reverie.

"Ooh honey, were you crying? I don't like this marshy side of yours, baby," Omari said, holding her.

"It is just that Sandra went through a lot, and it hurts me that people who caused it all are just walking freely back in the village. It breaks my heart to pieces." She said sadly, letting tears to flood her face.

"I will go back to the village in two weeks' time to see to it that that man is behind bars. I have done a background check and I am told he has a stepbrother who protects him in high places. But I have that covered as well. They want to play rough; I will smear it up in cement for them," Omari growled.

"Thank you, love. I don't know what I would be without you." Zari said.

"It is okay. I promised to take care of you. What are you going to do about the land?" He asked.

"I don't know yet. It belongs to Sandra. Maybe I will suggest that we build an orphanage there or a shelter for girls who face molestation, and they have no one to take care of them," Zari said.

"That is a good idea," Omari remarked. "Your mother would be very proud of you."

"Mommy, can I accompany big brother next week to Sandra's school? I want to see the beautiful girls in her school too," Omari Junior busted into the room.

Both parents were startled. Omari was the first to react, for Zari had to hide her teary face from her son.

"It is okay, son. You can join him. On one condition…"

"No conditions, dad," OJ said. His father smiled. OJ was more like his mother.

"Now go tell your aunty to open the main door. Your uncles and aunties are already here. The boy ran out, smiling.

Dinner was beyond Zari and Sandra's expectations. Guests were in a jubilant mood. The food was amazing. Sandra kept a respectful silence and only spoke when spoken to. She wore a long dress and had her hair covered like Zari and the rest of the women and girls. She was able to talk to some, and she noticed that her brothers came to her defense every time anyone said anything mean to her. She felt so safe and secure. Even the dreadful Ahmed, her eldest grandfather, smiled at her. Her mother had prepared her on what to expect. She knew it would be hard blending in but Zari had promised that with time, she would learn their language and attend classes that make her one of them. Sandra was willing and ready. Having two cultures wasn't so bad. Zari had done it and she was going to do it better than her mother.

CHAPTER NINETEEN

Dogs of the Same Street Bark Alike...

School looked different. It had a warm, receptive smile that Sandra had never seen since she joined form one. It had always been cloudy, cold, and grey on opening days, but today was different. The birds sang melodiously, sending their sweet tweets in the air like a trained chorale. The sky was sparkling blue with brushes of clouds here and there along the horizon. Butterflies migrated in a swarm of shiny cream, flapping their wings faintly as if to send whispers of hope to the trio that had just arrived on the compound. There were two men and a girl. There was a brown girl with straight dark hair that was held in a knot, as if to stop the waves from cascading down her shoulders. Sandra stepped onto the gravel that carpeted the car park and listened to the smash between the two dark nemeses, her new Bata toughees pair of shoes, and the tarmac spread on the parking square. She let down the second foot and stood straight like she was sending a message to the peepers that she had arrived.

She did not have to look in the direction of the classroom to know that eyes and jaws were dropping on her. She had done it herself in admiration of the daughters of ministers who arrived in posh slithering vehicles, some dark, others shiny, making wishes that one day she would take her child to school in one. Sandra never imagined that one day, in the nearest future, she would be one of them. She would be talking the language of the streets, waiting in a jam, knowing buses and their numbers, street names and many more fancy things about living in the city. She was one of them. She had a handsome brother, Arabic, with the color of white coffee and hair that needed no brushing, a driver who would be driving her to school and picking her up every opening and closing day. For a moment, Sandra stopped and looked towards the heavens. She wanted to shout into the sky, send an enormous thank you to God, but she only closed her eyes for a moment and walked on towards the administration block. Hussein stayed behind the driver as Sandra led the way towards the front. She walked with an exaggerated swing. She was very proud of her new self.

"Excuse me, madam," she cooed, "I have reported back from home."

The secretary, a heavy breathing woman, looked up to see the transformation of a girl who had been one of the most pitied in form two, a few days ago. She had been gone for a week, and things were so different. Her hair had grown so fast. She looked pretty in her new uniform and shoes. Her eyes were brighter than the stars. *And who was the boy in her company?* They had a distant resemblance, like cousins. *What about the man carrying her luggage?* Things were not adding up, and the more she thought about it, the more her jaw dropped.

"Nakhumicha! Is that you?!" the secretary asked with shock written all over her face, picking up her jaw before it hit the floor.

The woman's eyes were so dilated that tiny red capillaries could be seen running all over her ever-white cornea. Her long lashes, heavy with mascara, flapped in coordination with her slowly gaping thick lower lip that looked heavier in red lipstick. Sandra smiled at her and frowned at the name "Nakhumicha."

It had escaped her that in school, many people knew her as Sandra Nakhumicha, the girl who was very clever but had no parents. The girl whose grandmother had recently died. The girl whose name appeared on every scholarship and bursary that the school got. The girl on the pity lips of both teachers and students, especially when just a week ago the school had sent a delegation of teachers and a few students to pass a message of condolence only to find the directed place locked and deserted, two days after the burial. A team of village women had been sent to receive the delegation and made some sugarless tea for them, discovering the poverty that Nakhumicha had been raised in. Teachers could not wrap a finger around what had happened to their genius girl, so they asked around for a village elder. Mzee Kapanga, in his usual composure and clarity, explained to them about the girl having been taken to the city where her mother was to keep her safe from her father and his cruelty. Having taken the sugarless tea escorted by a buzz of fat dark flies, the group left the village, without seeing the girl who brought them to the village but with a cocktail of feelings about her wellbeing.

Nakhumicha returned to school with a new name and status. Her past was buried with her grandmother. Her dreams of being a lawyer like her mother, were fanned and now had caught flames. Her eyes were focused on the goal, especially after her mother reminded her that she will always be a village girl if she doesn't stand out and work harder than the rest.

"The city does not change your status honey," her mother had said softly just above the humming juicing machine. "It is a place of hidden opportunities for the likes of us, you will have to dig deeper than those born and raised here. You and I are not."

They were making her farewell dinner, the evening before she went back to school. Sandra had requested her new parents to allow her to continue in her old school because it was the only place she fit in comfortably. Beneath the main reason, it was her only chance of seeing Dau again. Zari had talked to her at length, couching her on Islam and blending in with the rest to avoid stigma. She had asked Sandra to consider learning Arabic after form four, but Zari promised to let her wear whatever she wanted. The family practiced Islam but embraced modernity at all costs. Zari herself wore *buibui* and *hijab* only on special Islamic occasions and when visiting Omari's Eldest brother who insisted on her covering up so as not to expose the *other half* that she was.

Her mother was right. The city did not take away one's true identity. It only elevated her to a position that played no role to her future or status in reality. Sandra understood that she was still a village girl and had to stand out from the rest. Her mother made it clear to her that she had to be exceptionally smart to survive in the new community that was adopting her. Sandra kept these rules at heart and recited them before going to bed. She believed in God and Jesus but kept her faith to herself, just like her mum had warned.

"No one needs to know what you believe in. keep it silent and nobody will bother you," Zari had said, lowering her voice. "Omari and I could become anything we want but his family ties us down. Your brothers are also sunken into the beliefs of their people, be careful what you say around them."

"Yes mum," Sandra responded, handing over the chopped onions and tomatoes. It was very natural, calling her mummy. She loved the time they spent in the Kitchen together.

It was going to be a long term but filled with fun. It had kicked off on the right note for now. Even so, girls from town wanted to be her friends. Sandra stayed closer to Nelly, her high school best friend. Nelly was not very beautiful. She had a flat face like a bush baby with a forehead that ended too soon, allowing hair to curl alongside her face. Nelly's eyes were clear and small, looking like tiny pearls in the sand. She always had a smile or a blush on her wide plane of a face. She was timid and very discreet. Their poverty and brains had brought them together.

Tabby, on the other hand, did not know how to approach the current Sandra. She used her position as a prefect to maneuver around Sandra, but she managed to keep her at bay. Tabby's long hair, always up in a bouncy ponytail, her long chiseled legs and chocolaty skin that was always coconut-scented left many girls brimming with envy, but not Sandra. Tabby was bold and talked to any teacher in any manner. Many girls believed she got favors because her father was a huge politician who ensured lots of bursary funds came to Weledi Girls School. They also thought that since Sandra had new status, she would automatically become friends with her. They were wrong.

"*Weee, staki shida na serikali...*" Most of the girls responded to Tabby's advances whenever she tried befriending them. Sandra was not about to make the mistake of befriending Tabby, even with her new status.

Sandra longed for a symposium or any outing to any School. She wanted to see Dau. She wanted to tell him how things had changed for her. She wanted to tell him about her mum and how it was so beautiful in the city. That evening, before she settled into a group discussion for mathematics, she picked up her writing pad. She chose this writing pad carefully in the supermarket during her first time shopping spree and kept it carefully just for Dau. It was pink, stripped with hearts and splashes of fairies all over. She wrote Dau a letter with a smile on her light face. This time she had stamps ready, new and unused.

> *Well Ghee*
> *Box private bag,*
> *Kijijini*
>
> *My love Dau,*
>
> *How have you been? I want to take this opportunity to put my feelings on paper to let you know that my heart stopped beating the day we parted. I have really missed you.*
> *Did you hear about my grandmother? I wish you were there. I went to cry at the dam without you. I am still very sad. Anyways, I have good news and bad news.*
> *I found my mum, Dau. She is very beautiful! I hope you will one day meet her. My grandfather has decided to adopt me, so I am like the daughter they never had. I have three brothers and they are very handsome. But not more handsome than you.*

I really don't know how we will continue. My life in the village is ended so I won't be seeing you over the holidays. But I will work hard to join the university.

Will you be going for the mathematics symposium in Imara High? I hope I will see you there. I really miss you my love. It breaks my heart every time I think about you.

Say hi to all your friends, especially Denny and Alibaba. Goodbye until we meet again. I will always love you.

Dedications: I miss you by Aaliyah.

Your love,
Michaa.

The letter was sealed with tears of a desperate longing and drops of perfume. She posted the letter the following day, carrying the dreams and the hopes of a love that only Sandra understood.

It did not take long before the dates for the symposium popped up on the school calendar. Sandra, together with other science students in school, were busy ironing the blouses and skirts for the outing. Sandra stayed in the corner, using the old iron box to fix her outfit. Meanwhile, Tabby with her Town crew, used modern iron boxes to straighten their piped skirts.

"I heard there is a new kid on the block," Tabby mouthed the words with an exaggerated sneer on her face, dropping a look at Sandra.

"Be careful what you say around some people, Tabby," one of her puppets Belinda, replied, "She is the new 'Principal's Mouth'."

Sandra wanted to jump on them. She knew they were referring to her because they had seen her be summoned to the principal's office. The principal had called on Sandra to ask about her whereabouts with her new family. However, rumors had spread about her being a snitch. It took her by surprise, but the events of the last few days had made her forget about it.

Sandra was so exhausted with how the so-called Town Crew treated the other girls like second class students. She wanted them to know that there was nothing wrong with being a village girl or coming from a humble background. Sandra wanted to make it clear that all girls were the same and nothing made the other different, just because their parents had money. Each one came to make a future for themselves. Sandra's mouth parted, her face screwed in response- but Nelly, pinched her hard. It was a signal to keep her silent because there was no use starting a fight with the other group.

"Girls, let's walk to the bus, please. Ensure you have full school uniform on," Mrs. Obabu said through the window, sending all of them scrambling out, trying to tuck in their shirts and tighten their ties at the same time.

Going out with Mrs. Obabu meant they were going to have fun. After all, Mrs. Obabu cared more about her colleagues from other schools and sharing the greatness of Weledi Girls than watching over the girls and forcing them to stay in the bus like other teachers did.

Dau had not replied to Sandra's letter and it bothered her. She wanted to find out if everything was okay with him. Like any other teenager in love, her mind was decorated with moons and stars about him and any threat caused dark clouds. The sky above her was however all clear and no cloud threatened her sky. The birds flew rhythmically in the air and the insects chirruped, even during the day. The thought of Dau, his look, the way he touched her arm, how he pulled her in his arms when saying goodbye, the talks by the dam, made her world spin. She closed her eyes, shutting out the noise of her fellow students and the humming of the bus. Sandra drifted into a fantasy that painted her light face pink. Her velvet soft cheeks bloomed like rose petals.

In her fantasy, she sees Dau come to her while she is sitting at their favorite spot at the dam. The water is crystal clear, not the usual muddy yellowish ripples. Sandra can see the soft round stones at the bottom of the dam, sparkling as a kaleidoscope of rays from the evening sun smooch the clear surface of the dam. He sprints towards her, his arms stretched, open to swallow her petite form in a warm hug that always lingers on for a little longer. But as he comes, another form jumps out, looking like a mermaid as it shoots from the clear water. The calm and the sparkle disappears and is replaced with rowdy muddy ripples. Dau stares at the mermaid and starts walking towards it. He does not hear as Sandra calls after him. He stretches his hand towards the mermaid, and she takes it, pulling him back in the water. Sandra screams for help but the mermaid laughs louder, drowning her screams. The mermaid has Tabby's face and hair.

"Sandra, we are here! Look, the Boys' School has arrived already!" Nelly jerked her out of her agonizing reverie.

"Ooh!" Sandra tried, wearing a bold face, "I hope Dau is here."

It was more of like a plea than a statement. Her head had been thrown into the confusion. And the concepts she had studied in preparation for the symposium were gone. All she wanted to see was Dau and from him, get an assurance that he still loved her.

The events of the day ran in her eyes like a scratched DVD. The facilitators and teachers who addressed the students on various topics in science were scratchy and noisy. She wanted them to stop talking. Dau had not looked for her and she thought she saw him walk Tabby out during lunch break. He had totally ignored her.

When the session finally came to an end and teachers asked students to wait in their various buses, her fears were confirmed. Dau and Tabby walked past her, hand-in-hand. Sandra's heart hit against her ribs and it hurt like a blunt stab. She could suddenly not breathe. Sandra thought she was going to die. When Nelly held her hand, Sandra did not notice. When she told her to move to the bus, Sandra heard nothing. When Nelly told her, she was attracting a crowd, she heard incoherent whispers. So, Nelly dropped her hand and walked to the bus with the hope of finding some boy to walk her there. No one had ever asked Nelly to be his girlfriend. It worried her but she was grateful at the same time because she did not have to go through the pain Sandra was going through. She also hoped that her friend would get over what she had seen and go back to being herself. She had never seen Sandra that distraught.

Having no one asking them out at the age of sixteen would give any girl worries. Nelly had not received any proposals. She worried sometimes but regularly talked about the right time as the women in school kept her going. Even though other girls who already had boyfriends were struggling with keeping the puppy flame ablaze, Nelly found high-school relationships time-wasting. She knew her time would come, and a tall, dark, handsome boy would ask her to be his girlfriend. Nelly promised herself that Sandra would be the first to know when it happened, just like she had trusted her with everything about Dau.

Sandra found an empty chair in the classroom and sank in it. Her world came crashing on her head. She felt the dam rise and swallow her, the moon dropped and cracked her skull, and the smooth stones at the bottom of the dam stood sharply and penetrated her smoothening soles. Sandra's heart bled furiously. It was broken. She had never experienced such pain. Her chest did not hurt like it did when Granny died; it was her heart. It hurt so much she couldn't breathe. She wanted to cry but no tears came, her lips were dry, and her throat felt croaky.

"Micha, why are you sitting here alone?" his voice startled her.

She thought it was in her, head playing tricks on her or something.

"Micha, are you okay?" Dau asked again.

She found little strength to look up and there he stood, his face a splash of worry. *Does he have any idea the kind of pain he is causing me? Does he know what I feel? How can he stand there and ask me if I am okay?* Sandra's pain turned into a deep resentment. Tears stung her eyes and when she opened her mouth to answer him, it just trembled. She had never felt so vulnerable. She wanted to throw desks, chairs and papers at him.

"What's wrong Micha? Are you okay?" Dau wanted to hold her.

He had never seen her like this. Her face was a squelch of horrid pink. Tears and mucus coated her smooth cheeks, making them slimy. He did not know what to say so he just sunk in the empty chair that was next to her and waited. The ten minutes were like ten years for Dau.

When he had walked out, after the symposium, Sandra was talking to Nelly and she looked happy. The girl from her school, Tabby had just grabbed his hand and pulled him out. He had no idea why she did that, but he knew that Sandra would wait for him in the hall. He came back after struggling to shake off the sticky girl and there she was, all pink, teary and sulking. What had happened? Had someone offended her? Was she sick? He could not wrap his thick fingers around whatever bothered her. Sandra wiped her face with a clean handkerchief from her pocket, looked around the empty hall and slowly stood up. She had grown taller and her frame had gathered some weight. Dau caught the scent of perfume that had replaced her old tiptop-body-jelly. It was mild and feminine mixed in her own sweat. His heart raced.

He pulled the only card he knew would tell him the truth. "Are you breaking up with me?" He asked. "I know you have moved to the city and maybe you don't want anything to do with me. I will understand. But I want you to know that I love you so much, Micha."

His heart stopped for a moment when the words came out. He did not know what to say to her. For a moment, he thought he saw a sparkle in her eyes. Then, suddenly, like someone bitten by a wasp, she pulled out her hand, slapped him on the face and stormed out.

For a few seconds, Dau was mortified. *What has just happened? What has the city done to my Micha?* He loved the new version, though.

His finger sought his face and touched the feeling that was flaring on his cheeks. He slowly walked out, to catch her disappearing into a corner.

When Sandra stepped in the bus, Tabby was doing a head count. She glared at Tabby, found her seat next to panicky Nelly and settled in.

"Where have you been, Sandra?" Nelly asked, her voice quivering.

"In the hall." Sandra responded consciously, afraid of her burning rage. She had never felt what she was feeling, and she did not know how to place it. Her belly was in knots, her breath was warm, and it felt like some good fever. He had said he loved *her*, not Tabby. Was that what jealousy felt like? Where did that slap come from? Dau's surprised face made her chuckle.

"Are you okay?" Nelly asked, edging closer to her friend. She had never seen Sandra like that. Her ears were pink, and her lips were swollen. Though she had left shock-stricken, her eyes had a different kind of glow.

"I am fine, Nelly. Just shocked." Sandra tried sounding normal.

"You were wrong Sandra, he loves you," Nelly said, reading her mind.

"I don't know Nelly, they walked out holding hands," Sandra whispered carefully, lest the keen ears from town catch her words.

"No. she had pulled him out. I found Dau telling the Witch to stop bothering him and that he loved only you," Nelly almost shouted.

Sandra pinched her and she squirmed in her seat. Nelly got the message. Such matters were supposed to be said in whispers. Sandra felt her heart warm up. She smiled in contentment then asked if Nelly was sure. Nelly confirmed with a nod and Sandra unconsciously reached for her hand. It felt like how it was with Timina, her childhood friend. She suddenly missed Timina. She wondered what had become of her and silently prayed that she was okay. Sandra still hoped that one day they will meet. There was a lot they had to exchange. Sandra looked at Nelly and there it was! The excitement of gossip. Nelly's eyes were twinkling with curiosity. She looked like she wanted to know what had transpired.

"I slapped him, Nelly!" Sandra whispered, after looking around.

"Whaaaat!" Nelly almost shouted, "Tell me! Tell me! Tell me everything!

Sandra did not know how to explain it. She just smiled and pressed hard against her friend, who squeezed her hand in return.

"You are so lucky Sandra," Nelly quipped after a short silence.

"Why? I just lost my grandma and am not even done mourning!" Sandra said, facing her friend. "And I just slapped my boyfriend after he confessed that he loved me."

"What do you mean? Losing your granny is sad but you finally met your mum, you have three handsome brothers, you have a rich grandfather who is going to be your dad, you have a handsome boyfriend who loves you. Now he knows better never to mess with your feelings. Girl, I want your life!" Nelly bubbled on about her friend's luck.

Sandra felt so good. She had never been so happy. Actually, Nelly was right, she *was* lucky.

CHAPTER TWENTY

Dark is the Eleventh Hour, but Morning Certainly Comes…

"Sandra. Sandra. Sandra wake up." Nelly called screaming. It was four in the morning. They were supposed to go to class for morning preps earlier than everyone else, but Sandra had not woken up.

"Help! Somebody help!" Nelly screamed again. There was a sudden commotion in the dormitory. Girls jumped off their beds and ran to Sandra's cubicle. Sandra's cubemates also woke up.

There was a 'What is wrong with her?' here and a 'What happened' there. The head girl was already asking some girl guides, "go and wake up the school nurse!"

Sandra's mouth was frothing.

"Oh my God, she is not breathing," Nelly said, throwing her hands on her head.

She was visibly crying. Other girls started crying too. There was a great pandemonium in the dormitory. The nurse came running, and the boarding mistress followed shortly after having heard the commotion and muffled screams of girls.

"What happened to her?" the nurse barked.

"I just went to wake her up but found her frothing at the mouth and not breathing," Nelly responded, crying.

"We need an ambulance," The nurse ordered the fierce boarding mistress for the first time.

"Let me call the principal first. We can use her car. An ambulance will take too long." The boarding mistress said. The head girl was busy trying to calm the other girls down.

A car was brought quickly, and Sandra was rushed to Mulukulu Mission Hospital, just across the school fence. Nelly accompanied the teacher and nurse. The doctors looked at Sandra once and declared that it was an emergency, and she was to be put on life support. Some blood samples were taken.

In the meantime, the principal called Omari and Zari, since they were the ones taking care of Sandra.

"She was poisoned," the doctor announced to the weary faces sitting at the waiting lounge at daybreak. "She ingested battery acid, and one of her kidneys and a huge part of her liver are really damaged. Maybe you should call the police. It might be a case of attempted suicide."

"No! No! My daughter would never take poison," Zari said shrilly. Her eyes were suddenly wet. Omari was quickly by her side. They had left the house immediately. The principal called them, stating that Sandra was in the hospital. Omari had driven like a maniac, with Zari screaming at him to go faster.

"Sandra is not suicidal," Nelly said.

"Might you be aware of the last thing she ate?" the doctor asked.

"Yes," Nelly said, suddenly remembering the events of the previous evening.

"Tabby gave her some juice yester night as a peace offering. They had fought over…" her voice trailed off, when she remembered that it was wrong to fight over boys in school. Nelly worried about what Tabby could do to her. She did not want to lose her scholarship.

"It is okay. Go on," The doctor said.

"Maybe we need to go bring that Tabby girl here," Zari screamed.

"You need to calm down, madam. We have to inform the police first, and only the principal can do that," The doctor said. Zari's face was pink with horror. Omari held her tight.

"My girl is dying in there—my daughter. I just met her…" her voice dawdled off.

"Zari, she is not dying. Control yourself," Omari said, sternly.

"You don't understand. None of you understand," she was whimpering. Nelly was crying too.

"Go back to school and get the cup she drank in. Bring it here. Don't talk to anyone," the Principal instructed Nelly.

The police were already in the hospital. They recorded a statement with the doctor. When Nelly came back with the cup twenty minutes later, they took her statement too. It was confirmed in the laboratory that the cup had traces of acid.

Back in school, Tabby woke up excited, but started panicking when she was told Sandra was rushed to the hospital. She was silent for the first time. She did not talk to anyone. When the police car pulled up to pick her, she started screaming, daring them to touch her.

"You don't know who my father is. All of you will be fired," she screeched.

A female police officer walked her to the police car, and they drove off.

"But Daddy said it wouldn't kill her. I am not a murderer. Daddy said it would only teach her a lesson to keep off my boyfriend." Tabby went on screaming, as the officers recorded her rants.

At the Hospital, the principal was trying to explain to Zari and Omari who Tabby's father was.

"Is he the Minister in charge of Energy?" Omari asked.

"Yes," the principal said. "I am so scared. If he gets to know that his daughter was arrested, the whole school will shut down," the principal's voice was panicky.

Omari knew the reason behind Sandra's poisoning.

"Why would Sandra fight with that man's daughter?" Zari asked.

"It was not Sandra's fault. That man is Masafu's stepbrother. It must be his doing. I am sure that he used the girl to get back at us," Omari said.

"What are you talking about?" Zari asked her mouth tight and teeth clenched.

"Masafu was arrested. I just did not want to tell you before he is sentenced. I had to use officers from the city and a few friends. The minister threatened to retaliate. Thank God, I have his threats recorded. I just did not imagine..." Omari responded.

"Imagine what? That he will get back through Sandra? You should have told me. We could have warned the School," Zari flared up.

"I did not know the daughter was Sandra's School mate, honey," Omari pleaded.

The Principal had rushed to get a phone call and came walking back, trembling.

"He says he is on his way. The Minister is on his way. What have you people done to my school?" The principal panicked.

Omari said, "Don't worry, madam. I can call a few friends to ensure he is arrested before he comes here. I just wonder how he got to give Tabby the information so fast."

The principal responded, "He called her yesterday on my phone. He must have instructed her to do it. Plus, battery acid can be found anywhere on the school compound, especially in the physics laboratory. Tabby is a physics student."

"We need a kidney donor," the doctor announced. "It is the only way we can save the girl."

"I will do it," both Omari and Zari volunteered.

"I am her mother. I will give it," Zari said sternly. Omari knew better not to argue.

"We will have to run some tests to ensure it's the right fit," the doctor said to her.

"I'm sure it'll be the right fit. I'm her mother," Zari said back.

"When we get out of surgery, if I make it alive, please, Omari, I need to hear that the man behind this is behind bars. And the wretched daughter, too. I don't care who they are…" Zari ranted, crying. It had been two beautiful weeks, and now it was all gone. Her innocent daughter was fighting for her life, and she had to save her. Omari, on the other hand, had to ensure that the minister didn't win. It was dangerous but necessary. A man had to protect his family. He assured the principal that things would be under control.

The madam went to restore order in the school and explained why Tabby had been arrested to the nearby students, who were wild with curiosity. Nelly was made the school senior prefect as a reward for helping save Sandra's life.

The doctor tested Zari, and her kidney was a perfect match for her daughter's. This was a miracle; almost too good to be true. It seemed impossible.

The surgery took ten long hours. Omari worked closely with Ahmed, who at first refused to help him but later came in with his significant contacts to contain Tabby's father. He was intercepted before he reached school. It was all over the news. Omari also gave evidence that the minister smuggled bhang from the village. This was the last nail on his coffin.

"Mommy," Sandra whispered.

"My girl," Zari whispered back.

The doctor kept checking their vitals on the computer.

"The two of you are out of danger. But you will stay here for a week or so since you are too delicate to be moved," the doctor announced.

Mother stretched her hand and tried to touch her daughter, but her bed was too far.

"Be strong for me, baby," Zari whispered tears running down her face.

"It is okay, mom. We will be fine," Sandra tried, sounding confident. She had no idea what had happened. There was a dull pain in her stomach. She closed her eyes and willed her mind to wonder off.

The two women drifted to sleep with beautiful smiles on their faces. Together they were a winning team. Zari knew that her daughter would not object to going back to the village to build an orphanage for girls and a safety place for molested girls. Sandra dreamt about being a lawyer like her mother and ensuring that all those who abused girls and women faced justice. Sandra's smile deepened at the thought of walking down the aisle with Dau waiting for her in a captain's suit. He had said in his last letter that he wanted to study marine science in college. He had promised to love her forever.

END!